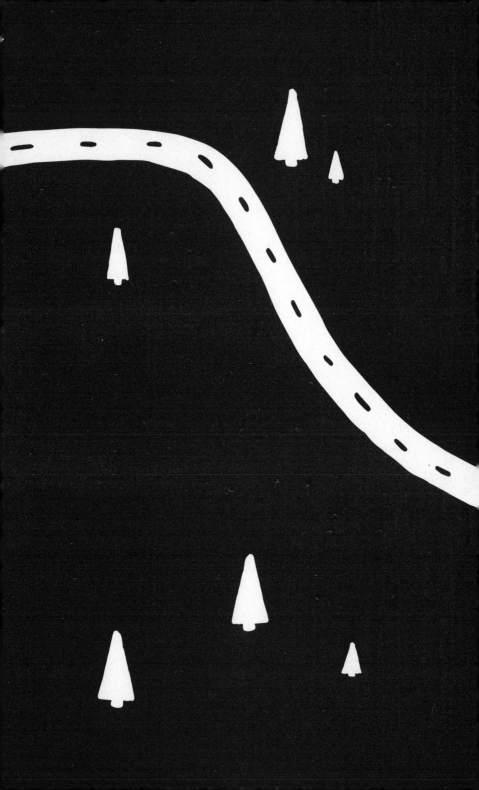

THE
HONEST
TRUTH

DAN
GEMEINHART

SCHOLASTIC PRESS / NEW YORK

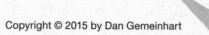

All rights reserved. Published by Scholastic Press, an imprint of Scholastic Inc., *Publishers since 1920*. SCHOLASTIC, SCHOLASTIC PRESS, and associated logos are trademarks and/or registered trademarks of Scholastic Inc.

Library of Congress Cataloging-in-Publication Data available

ISBN 978-0-545-66573-5

10 9 8 7 6 5 4 3 2 1   15 16 17 18 19

Printed in the U.S.A.   23

First edition, February 2015

Book design by Nina Goffi

FOR KAREN,
FOR EVERYTHING AND ALWAYS.

AND FOR MARK,
OFF TO MOUNTAINS NOW.

CHAPTER

1

MILES
TO GO:
263

The mountain was calling me. I had to run away. I had to. And I didn't need anyone to go with me.

I tightened the straps on my backpack and held the front screen door open with my foot. "Come on, Beau!" I called, and my voice didn't shake one bit. It was strong. Like me.

Beau came rocketing out the door, his tail slapping my legs. He danced on his front paws on the porch, his mismatched eyes smiling up at me, his tongue hanging out happy. I bent down and scratched him behind his ears the way he loved, the way only I knew how to do. "You're always ready for a walk, aren't you, buddy?"

He panted out a yes.

"Well," I said, grabbing the handles of my duffel bag and standing up. "You're in for a doozy." I looked out to the horizon, to the white-topped mountains in the distance. "The biggest walk of all. That's the truth."

I slammed the door behind me and I didn't look back even once. I didn't worry about a key. I might not ever be coming back.

Beau walked right up against my leg the whole ten minutes down to the station. My camera swung and thumped against my stomach, dangling from a strap around my neck. When I saw the station up ahead, I ducked around a corner and crouched down in an alley. My breath came in nervous puffs. "All right, Beau, now just like we practiced." I unzipped the duffel bag and spread it open. It was mostly empty. I patted the inside of it. "Come on, Beau. Get on in."

Beau stepped right in, spun around a couple of times, and then flopped down. He looked up at me. "God, you're a good dog," I whispered. His tail tried to wag inside the duffel. I fished in my pocket for a biscuit, and he snuffled it out of my hand in one chomping gulp.

I zipped the duffel almost all the way closed. Beau disappeared into the darkness inside. I stood up and Beau's weight pulled my shoulder down. I tightened my grip. "I'm glad you're not a Saint Bernard," I whispered down to the duffel bag, then walked out around the corner and up to the ticket window.

The man behind the window squinted up at me from the magazine he was reading. I straightened my bright red baseball hat and cleared my throat.

"I need two tickets," I said.

"Bus or train?"

"Bus. To Spokane."

"You traveling alone?"

The word *alone* rang like a broken bell. I licked my lips. "My dad's in the bathroom," I answered. "He gave me money for the tickets."

The man nodded and yawned. People are lazy. That's what I was counting on.

"Okay. One adult, one child, Wenatchee to Spokane. That's forty-four dollars."

I pulled the money out of the pocket of my blue jacket and handed it to him.

"Bus leaves in ten minutes from right over there."

I took the tickets and walked the way he'd pointed. A couple of buses were rumbling next to the curb. One said *Spokane* on the front, just like my tickets. I looked over my shoulder. The man behind the window had his eyes back down on his magazine. I walked right past the bus and around the corner of the building.

To the train platform.

There was the little covered seating area I'd seen when I'd made my plans. The one with the garbage can chained up behind it, mostly out of sight. I ducked around to the garbage can, took a quick look to make sure no one was watching, then slipped off my blue jacket and stuffed it into the garbage. My red hat and the two bus tickets went in after it. I grabbed the dark green wool winter hat out of my backpack and pulled it on.

When I turned to go, I felt the bulge in my pocket. I took a shaky breath and pulled out the watch. It was an old-fashioned silver pocket watch with a round glass face. A present from my dead grandpa. I bit my lip, hard. I could feel it ticking in my hand. *Tick. Tick. Tick.* Time, running out.

Here's what I don't get: why anybody would want to carry something around that reminds you that your life is running out.

I threw the watch to the ground as hard as I could. It smashed against the concrete. The glass cracked but didn't break. My jaw clenched and I stomped on it, so hard my foot hurt. The glass shattered, and I stomped again, and the clock hands bent. I stomped again, and again.

I had my foot raised for another stomp when I heard Beau whine from the duffel. My lungs were heaving. My breaths were hard and fast, and my stomach was starting to feel sick. A thin ache had begun to poke in my head. Beau whined again.

"It's okay, Beau," I panted, and lowered my foot. I reached down to throw the watch into the garbage can, but stopped. I looked at the garbage can, looked at the ruined silver watch. I straightened up and felt the camera against my body. I lifted it to my eye and snapped a picture of the broken pieces of watch lying scattered on the ground. Then I kicked them behind the garbage can.

When I walked around the corner I saw the train waiting. It was sleek and silver and rumbling like a bottled earthquake. I fished in the pocket of my gray hoodie and found my train ticket, the one I'd ordered online the night before with the credit card I'd snuck out of my mom's purse. My belly lurched.

"Heading to Seattle?" the lady asked when she took my ticket. I nodded and started to climb aboard. I didn't want her to remember me. "All by yourself? You need help with your bag?"

I tried not to give her a dirty look. "No," I said without looking at her, and climbed up the stairs onto the train, my legs and fingers burning with Beau's weight.

The train was mostly empty, and I found a seat in an empty row at the back of the car. Outside the big window was Wenatchee, the home I was leaving. The sky was getting dark. The low buildings and warehouses around the train tracks threw long shadows. The clouds were dark and heavy. A storm was coming, and so was night.

Somewhere out there in that darkness was Jessie, my best friend. And my mom, and my dad. Their faces floated into my mind. They had no idea I was leaving. They had no idea where I was going. They wouldn't be able to find me. They wouldn't be able to help.

I blinked my eyes hard and shook my head. "I don't need them," I whispered, squinting out at the town, the shadows. "I don't need anybody." It was true, maybe, but I didn't like how my words sounded more mean than strong. I touched the cold glass with my fingers, looking off into the distance toward the empty house my parents would come home to. "I'm sorry," I said even softer. "I'm sorry."

I pulled a little notebook and pen from the outside pouch of my backpack. I flipped past my homework and doodles and opened to the first empty page, then thought for a minute. I felt around in my head, trying to find the words for the moment. An idea came, slow and shy. I nodded. I counted a couple of times on my fingers, my mouth moving silently with the words. Then I wrote them down.

Outside, I heard the call: "All aboard!"

Then the rattling crash of a metal door closing.

I looked down at the words I'd written on the paper. Three lines:

Alone, leaving home.
A new journey, a new road.
Off to mountains now.

I slid my hand into the duffel bag on the seat beside me and found Beau's head. He licked my fingers. His tongue was wet, and his breath was warm. He felt soft. He felt like a friend. I scratched him behind his ears and tried not to cry. I tried hard to remember that I wasn't scared. Of so much.

I let my head fall back on the seat and tried not to think about anything but mountains.

In a couple of hours, my mom would get home.

A couple of hours after that, the police would start looking for me.

CHAPTER
1 ½

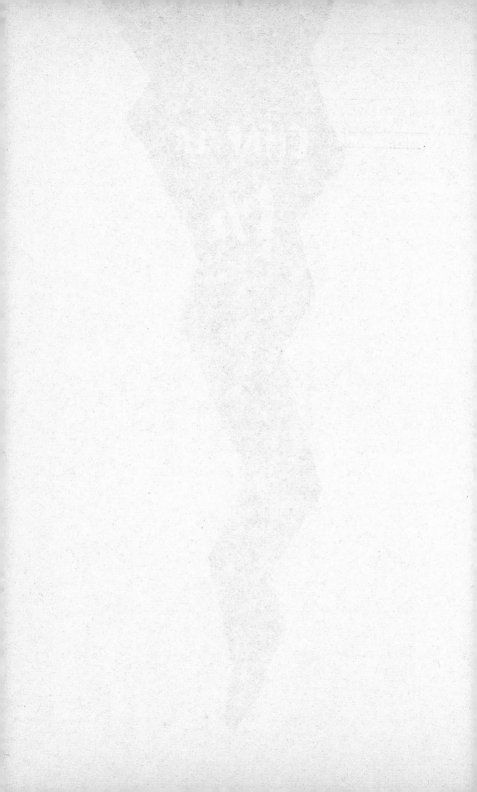

Her voice was shaky.

Like the last leaf in a tree.

Trying to hold on.

"Jessie, honey, is Mark over there? Is Mark with you?"

Jessica Rodriguez shook her head into the phone.

"Uh, no. I haven't seen him since school. What's the matter?"

"Oh," Mark's mom said, trying to laugh. Her laugh sounded more like a choke. "It's nothing, I'm sure. I was just surprised he wasn't home is all, and the house was so dark. . . ." Her voice trailed off. "Beau is gone, too. Let me know if he shows up there, would you?"

Mark never showed up.

The police don't usually come running when a kid's only been missing a couple of hours. But when his mom told them about Mark, about his story, they started listening a little more seriously. When they heard what the doctors had said, they listened real seriously. When they found the note he had left, they were completely serious.

So, a little after seven o'clock, two police cars raced into the parking lot by the bus station and train platform. They didn't have any real reason to think he'd gone there except that it looked like he was running away, and the only two ways for a kid to run away from Wenatchee were on the bus or the train. One of the cops jumped out of his cruiser and ran to the bus waiting there, a bus heading south to Oregon. He scanned the bodies in the seats, looking for a kid traveling alone. A skinny kid, with pale skin. A kid wearing a hat.

He didn't see one.

The other cop ran to the little window of the bus station and knocked on the glass. Behind the glass was a bored-looking man reading a magazine. He looked a little less bored when he saw it was a cop knocking.

The cop asked some questions, quick and sharp. The man licked his lips, scratched his chin, gave some answers. The cop nodded and walked back toward his cruiser, where he met his partner coming back from the bus. He opened his door and reached for the radio.

"Got him," the cop said.

"He's on the bus to Spokane.

"Wearing a red hat."

CHAPTER

2

MILES TO GO: 115

got off the train around nine o'clock. Alone in Seattle, with a whole dark night to get through. It was raining.

Once I got out of the station I set the duffel down and unzipped it. Beau came bounding out, his claws clattering on the wet sidewalk. His whole body was wagging.

"We got a long night ahead of us, Beauchamp." I scratched him behind the ears and slapped his ribs. "Our bus doesn't leave till tomorrow. There's a lot of time to kill." I slipped the backpack on. Beau scampered around, sniffing the strange city smells and going to the bathroom everywhere. Then we started walking.

The city was dark. It wasn't bright lights, lit-up buildings, cars, and people walking around like I'd imagined. The train station in Seattle was in the middle of empty warehouses and abandoned buildings. The streetlights were broken, mostly. The only people I saw looked homeless, curled up in doorways or coughing from the darkness of alleys. Beau growled at them and walked closer to my leg. Everything smelled like old cars and garbage.

In an hour I saw only a couple of cars go by. When I glimpsed the flash of their headlights and heard their tires crunching on the street, I ducked into whatever deep shadow I could find and tried to hold my breath. I gripped Beau's collar tight and whispered in his ear to calm him. The cops could be after me already.

As we passed a Dumpster, a crash sounded from the darkness behind it. A loud, metal crash like a garbage can getting knocked over. I screamed and jumped, my heart hammering. I almost dropped the empty duffel bag. Beau barked and the fur on his back raised. I almost started to run, but there was nowhere *to* run. There was a rustling sound in the darkness, like someone or something trying to get up. A scraping. Beau growled, low and deep in his throat, and backed up, his eyes on the noise. "Come on," I said, and my voice was shaking. We kept walking, faster. I looked back over my shoulder. Beau did, too. But whatever it was never left the shadows.

Block by block my legs got shakier. My stomach started getting wobbly and I kept swallowing spit. The little pain in my head got sharper. The backpack straps dug into my shoulders. I was too tired. I needed to rest. I needed to try to eat.

Beau wasn't wagging his tail anymore. His head turned back and forth, sniffing at every strange sound and looking at every black shadow. A growl lived down in his throat all the time. Everything felt like danger.

Ahead I saw the glowing windows of an all-night restaurant. It was a crappy place, the kind that has plastic ashtrays on the tables and serves breakfast all day. I felt the little bulge of money in my pants pocket. I didn't have extra, but I had just enough.

I dropped the duffel and spread it open. "Come on, buddy," I patted the bag. My words came between panting breaths. Beau's ears went back and his doggy eyebrows scrunched together. He whined and wagged his tail low. "I know," I said. "It sucks. But I'll get you some bacon." His ears perked up at the word. He tapped his toes a couple of times on the sidewalk and then stepped forward and curled up in the duffel. I scratched behind his ears before zipping him up.

My hands felt weak, like I couldn't make a fist, but I managed to lift the duffel. I looked at the darkness around me and walked into the restaurant.

The place smelled like stale cigarettes and coffee and frying eggs. Pictures flashed on a TV hanging in the corner, but the sound was off. My mouth started to water and my stomach woke up. Most of the tables were empty. There was an old couple chewing without talking at a corner booth, and a man with a long beard and ponytail sitting by himself at the counter. I wondered if he was homeless. A gum-chewing waitress was leaning against the counter, watching the TV. Everyone seemed tired and unhappy. The waitress looked me up and down.

"Just you?" she asked. Her voice was scratchy and rough. I nodded. "Pick any table you want, honey."

I slid Beau in his duffel into a booth and sat beside him. I left one hand on him to keep him still and opened a plastic menu with the other. I kept my backpack resting against my leg under the table. The city didn't feel safe. I was so tired the words on the menu blurred in my eyes.

"It's almost eleven o'clock." The waitress's voice in my ear made me jump. Her eyes glared questions at me. Through her caked-on makeup I could see the shadow of a black eye. Her mouth never stopped working on her gum. I blinked fast and nodded.

The chewing stopped. "So?" She raised her eyebrows and dropped her chin to look at me. "Whatcha doing out by yourself so late?"

My brain fumbled around for a good lie, but it was too tired; everything slipped out between its fingers. "I'm — not alone. My dad's, uh — out there." I nodded my head toward the window. The waitress squinted out into the darkness. Up the street, a neon sign glowed.

"What, at Barney's?" She rolled her eyes and shook her head. "Eleven at night and the guy's at a bar and his kid's eating at a diner. That's real sweet. Sounds like my dad." She looked down at me and her eyes were softer. Her teeth started in again on the gum. "Whatcha wanna eat, honey?"

"Toast. And scrambled eggs." I remembered Beau beneath my arm, lying in the darkness of the duffel. "And a side order of bacon. Please." The corners of the waitress's mouth curled up for just a second in what was probably supposed to be a smile.

"You got it."

My stomach growled and flopped while I waited. It was empty, but it wasn't exactly hungry. I was used to the feeling. The ache in my head had grown. It stabbed at my skull. I squinted my eyes against the pain, then reached into my coat pocket. My fingers closed around the plastic prescription pill bottle. I clenched my teeth, then pulled it out and opened it and rattled three of the pills into my hand. I got all three down with one gulp of ice water. I was a pro. I knew they'd make my head feel better.

But I hated the pills.

I slipped my hand inside the duffel to scratch Beau's ears. His soft, warm tongue licked my palm. He was such a good dog. Zipped up in a duffel bag, smelling food with an empty stomach, and he licks my palm. Tears burned uninvited into my eyes. Beau's love somehow stirred up all my sunken sadness. I bit my lip and looked out the window into darkness and tried to remember the last time I'd been happy.

I had to go back. Way back. Every memory for years was stained now, even the good ones. I had to go all the way back to before.

It was summer. Seven years ago. I was five.

Jess was over at my house, and we were playing in the backyard with Beau. He was just a puppy then, small and yippy and always tripping over his paws.

I'd felt good. Better. I didn't have a headache or anything.

We were running through the sprinkler. All the world was green grass and blue sky and shoulders hot with sunshine. We didn't have to have a reason to laugh.

Little kids are so dumb. They don't know anything yet. That's the truth.

My mom was on the back porch, sipping a glass of lemonade and watching us, a small smile on her face. I wonder if it was her last happy memory, too.

We laid down on the wet grass to catch our breath. We giggled and looked at the clouds. We compared belly buttons. Mine was an outie, pale and white. Jess's was an innie, a little crater in her light brown skin. Beau flopped down happily between us, filling our noses with the smell of wet dog.

"Look," Jess had said, propping herself up on one elbow. "Beau's kinda us put together."

I'd giggled.

"No, really. See?" She poked her fingers in his fur. "He's got two colors of fur. Brown, like your hair, and black like mine."

"Yeah," I'd said. I'd had shaggy brown hair. Sitting in the restaurant, I slid my hand up under my hat and felt my head.

"And his eyes," she'd continued. "One green," she said, pointing at it closely with a chewed fingernail. Beau squinted and turned his head away from her finger. "Like yours. And one brown," she finished, trying to point at his other eye. "Like mine."

I liked that idea. I liked it a lot. I had laughed out loud I liked it so much.

"He's like both of us," I said through a summer smile. "Together."

But at that moment, the phone rang. My mom jumped up to answer it. Fast.

I watched her go inside. I watched through the window as she picked up the phone and held it to her ear. I looked down at my belly button and the shimmering crystal of water pooled there.

"You think that's my *mamá* calling?" Jess asked, sitting all the way up and looking in at my mom.

"No," I'd answered, still looking down at my belly button. I reached out and petted my new puppy, scratched behind his ears and under his chin. He closed his eyes happily. He really seemed to like being scratched behind his ears. He was my dog.

God, I already loved him so much.

I saw, out of the corner of my eyes, Jess's body stiffen.

"Oh," she'd said. "Mark. Why's your mom crying?"

And that's where the happy memory stopped.

I thought of Jessie. Back home. She probably knew by now. She'd probably figured out where I was going. She'd probably figured out why. For some reason, that made me feel a little better. Like Beau and I weren't all alone. I pictured her brown eyes, how serious and deep they were, how she could look right into me in her quiet way and make me feel better. I closed my eyes for a moment and tried to feel her.

There. There she was. I smiled, just a little, to myself. That's the kind of friend she was. We were so together that we weren't ever really apart.

I pulled the notebook out of my backpack and started writing without thinking, stopping only for a second to count and make sure.

> *Across far, dark miles*
> *a friend can still hold your hand*
> *and be there with you.*

I read it over, then nodded. It worked. The thought of Jess made me feel better, but I couldn't shake the memory of my mom crying. I knew she was probably crying right at that moment. My dad, too, maybe. I'd seen way too much of them crying. That's the truth. My breath started shaking, and I gritted my teeth, pushing their faces away from my mind. Thinking of them wouldn't do me any good.

The waitress bumped out the kitchen door with a plate of food.

"Sorry, Willy, it ain't for you," I heard her say to the homeless-looking guy at the counter. "Earl says you gotta have money for food. You're lucky I'm giving you the coffee." She slouched over to where I sat.

"Here you go, honey." She slid the plate in front of me. The eggs didn't look anything like the way my mom made them. The crusts hadn't been cut off the toast like she did, either. "You gonna take your hat off and stay awhile?"

I looked up at her and her smacking lips. I wanted to yank the gum out of her mouth and throw it across the room.

"No."

She shrugged. "Suit yourself, sweetheart," she said through her gum, and walked away.

With a quick look around I grabbed the bacon and slipped it into the duffel bag. Beau's tongue slapped it out of my hand with hungry licks. I coughed to cover the slurping noises.

I got both pieces of toast down and still felt okay. I swallowed and looked at the runny eggs and tried to pretend they looked good. I needed to eat.

The first rubbery bite stuck in my throat, but I got it down. The second bite went down easier, but my stomach started to twitch and wiggle. I was chewing on the third bite when I saw what was on the TV.

At the top of the screen were the words, *Breaking News.* Beneath that was a map of the state of Washington, with a blinking red dot right in the middle marked *Wenatchee.* Where I'd run from.

At the bottom of the screen, in bold yellow letters, it said, *Missing Child Alert.*

My jaw stopped in mid-bite. My stomach clenched like a punching fist.

As I watched, they highlighted a wiggly line on the map. The line snaked from the red dot of Wenatchee to a new red dot labeled *Spokane.* The ghost of a smile tugged at the corners of my mouth. My trick had worked.

My smile dropped, though, at what came on the screen next. At the top of the screen was my name. At the bottom of the screen was a phone number. In the middle of the screen, taking up almost the whole TV, was a picture of me. It was my school picture. My red hat was on my head and I was grinning a big stupid smile. I hated that picture.

My eyes darted to the other people in the restaurant. No one was looking at the TV. I tried to swallow my bite of egg but it stuck in my mouth. I felt sick. My eyes flashed back and forth between the TV and the other customers. *Don't look up*, I prayed. My own smiling face on the TV teased me. *You can't get away*, it seemed to say. I ignored it and waited for the image to change. "Come on, come on," I whispered. How long were they gonna keep my picture up? Wasn't anything more important happening than some dumb kid running away?

The waitress walked out of the swinging door from the kitchen, a pot of coffee in her hand. She smacked her gum and walked over to the counter. She was facing right at the TV and my dorky school picture. I held my breath. She walked around behind the counter and set the coffee down, then started counting money from her apron pocket. The TV was right above her head. I was frozen, hardly breathing, with my mouth stuck open and my stomach flopping like a fish in the bottom of a boat.

She looked up from her money and saw me. I couldn't help it; my eyes flickered up to my picture behind her. She stopped chewing her gum and turned her head to look. My stomach caved in.

Just as her head made it almost all the way around, the picture changed back to the map. It still said *Missing Child Alert* on the screen, but my face was finally gone. I stared, breathless, at the back of the waitress's head. Had the picture changed before she'd seen it? My fist strangled the empty fork in my hand.

The waitress turned back to me and cocked an eyebrow. She put her money away and walked over to me, her gum smacking in her mouth. She put one hand on her hip and looked down at me.

"Missing kid, huh?" She leaned down a bit and lowered her voice. "Tell the truth, honey. Did that scare you?" I looked up at her, mouth still open, unable to speak. All my plans were gonna go up in smoke the first night, over a plate of runny eggs. "Well," she went on, "don't let it. There's more good folks than bad in the world, believe it or not. I bet they find him." She winked at me, and I tried desperately to smile.

She hadn't seen.

"I know it's tough," she added with a roll of her eyes out the window toward the neon bar sign. "Having a daddy who ain't really looking out for you." She reached down and patted my hand. "He don't know what he's missing out on, sweetie. And you're gonna be just fine. My dad was a bum, and I turned out all right."

She turned and walked away, and I finally started to breathe again. She didn't suspect a thing. I shook my head and took a shaky breath. People can be so blind. That's the truth.

The phone number was still on the TV, below the map. I grabbed my pen and wrote it on a napkin and shoved it in my pocket. I noticed the map had changed. Now, after the word *Spokane*, there was a question mark. Three more dots appeared on the red wiggly line between Wenatchee and Spokane. They were labeled *Quincy*, *Moses Lake*, and *Ritzville*. Of course. The bus had shown up in Spokane by now, and I wasn't on it. So they figured I must have gotten off at one of the stops in between. They were still off my trail.

As I closed my notebook, the nausea hit me: a green, rolling wave of sickness that started deep in my belly and rose up toward my throat. I grabbed the edge of the table with both hands, trying to ride it out.

It was no use. I knew the feeling too well. My mouth went dry, then filled with spit, then went sour. I jumped up and ran for the bathroom. I saw the waitress watch me from across the restaurant.

I barely made it. I planted my knees in front of the toilet just as my eggs and toast came back up. I tried to be quiet, but there's only so much you can do. My stomach heaved, and I lost all the food I'd managed to choke down. My eyes watered, and my hands shook. The floor was filthy. The toilet was already disgusting before I got there and it wasn't getting any prettier. Between heaves I spit and tried to breathe through my mouth and read all the dirty words scratched on the chipped metal walls of the bathroom stall. I thought of hungry Willy at the bar, and me puking up dinner.

Life sucks. That's the truth. Here's what I don't get: Why does everyone always try to pretend that it doesn't?

I rinsed my mouth in the sink and hurried back to my table. Beau, thank god, was still in the duffel. I'd been afraid he'd try to come and find me. I scratched him quick behind his ears and was zipping the duffel back closed when the waitress came up behind me.

"You okay, honey? Do you want some 7Up or something?" Her voice was all sweet and worried. Like a mom's. It only made me madder.

"No," I said without looking at her. "I just need to pay." I reached into my pocket and pulled out my wad of cash.

"Are you sure? I could get you some more toast, or go get your dad, or —"

"I'm fine," I snapped, and this time I looked at her. I could feel the anger in my eyebrows. Her eyes widened in surprise. "My dad gave me money for the food. Just give me the bill so I can go."

"You know what, honey, don't worry about it. Keep the money and don't tell your dad. Maybe it'll be helpful later."

"I don't need your help. I'm fine. I just need to pay and go. Tell me how much." My voice sounded angrier than I wanted, but my stomach was still gurgling and my legs were weak and the smell of coffee and bacon was making me feel worse and Beau was still stuck in the duffel. I wanted to get outside into the darkness so I could hug my dog and smell nothing except his fur. I wanted to get away from the TV.

The waitress snapped her gum a few times, then nodded. "It's eight bucks."

I pulled a ten and a twenty out of my handful of bills and dropped them on the table.

"That's enough for mine," I said. "And for whatever Willy wants." The world was starting to spin again and the taste of throw-up in my mouth wasn't making me feel any better. I shoved my notebook and pen into my backpack, grabbed Beau's duffel, and brushed past the waitress toward the door. I swallowed and breathed tight little breaths to keep from puking again.

The waitress followed me to the door.

"You're an angry kid," she said to my back as I pushed the door open. "But maybe you got reasons."

"Maybe I do," I answered, and the door closed behind me.

Outside, in the darkness, the cool air cleared my head. My stomach started to settle down. But I was still mad. Mad at the TV. Mad at my stomach. Mad at the waitress. I wasn't even sure why.

I walked out to the edge of the parking lot, to the end of where the light from the windows reached. I counted my stack of hard-saved money one more time, then slipped it back into my pocket. I turned around and looked at the restaurant. Dribbles of rain sprinkled down onto my neck.

Somewhere not too far away in the darkness a car alarm started screaming. The restaurant looked warm and cheerful, its yellow light spilling out like a runny egg yolk into the darkness. It looked safe, a place to come in from the cold. I could see the waitress clearing the dishes from my table, talking over her shoulder to the old couple. It was a place with sound and people, a place where life just kept going on. I hated it. I was standing outside, weak and tasting like vomit. Alone, again.

I lifted the camera from around my neck, framed the lighted windows of the restaurant right in the middle with the night's blackness all around, and snapped a picture.

I didn't see the gang of guys watching me from the shadows.

When I turned and walked away through the litter and broken glass of the empty, middle-of-the-night street, they were following close behind.

CHAPTER

2½

His family waited.

Silent and still by the phone.

Wanting their boy home.

Jessie waited with them. In plenty of important ways, she was a part of their family, too. They sat in the living room, faces pale and hands nervous and mouths tight. Silence was all around them, the phone most of all. Mark's mom was almost never not crying, though she cried without making a sound. She'd gotten very good at crying quietly.

Eight o'clock had come and gone, the time when the bus was supposed to arrive in Spokane. The cops were certain Mark was on that bus, and they were ready to greet it in the station. But the phone hadn't rung. It should have. It should have rung, and then a strong voice should have told them that they had Mark and that he was safe. But it didn't ring. Not until 8:15. And then a troubled voice had told them that the bus had pulled into Spokane, but Mark wasn't on it. He was gone, again. Mark's mom had dropped her face to her hands. His dad swore under his breath and pressed his fingers into his eyes.

Jessie had frowned, and squeezed her hands together, and wrestled with an idea. It was an idea that had started to whisper in her head the moment she'd heard that Mark was gone, but she'd ignored it. Mark had gotten on a bus to Spokane, after all. Her idea didn't make sense.

But with the bus in Spokane and Mark not on it, her idea got louder. It tugged on her sleeve and elbowed at her thoughts.

The cops were scrambling now. The bus had stopped in three towns between leaving Wenatchee and arriving in Spokane. The driver, tired and bored, hadn't paid attention to who had gotten off. They'd called the police in all three towns, and in all three towns every cop on duty was driving and looking, trying to find a small boy traveling with a little spotted dog. He had to be in one of those towns, the cops said. They'd call when they found him. Try not to worry.

Mark's dad was quiet. He looked exhausted. Mark's mom was crying again.

Jessie looked out the window. The idea inside her cleared its throat and poked her.

She didn't know it all yet. She hadn't learned what Mark had learned, hadn't discovered the secret that had made Mark pack his bag and disappear into darkness. If she had, the idea inside her would have kicked and stomped and grown into a rock-hard truth.

But then another idea came to her. She couldn't believe she hadn't thought of it before now. As soon as it came to her, she knew. She knew Mark would never leave without telling her good-bye.

"I've gotta go," she said, and was up and out the door.

She ran down the street, through the blowing wind and drizzling rain and darkness to her own house. She ran past the front porch and around the corner to the bricks beneath her bedroom window. Even in the darkness her hands had no trouble finding the loose brick, the one with the secret little empty space behind it. They'd been using it for years, her and Mark. A secret place only they knew about, a place they used to share secrets and pass notes.

Her finger poked back into the hole. Instead of brick, it felt paper. She bit her lip and pulled out the folded note.

A secret message.
Unfolding papers whisper.
A friend's last good-bye.

CHAPTER 3

MILES TO GO: 115

I heard their footsteps behind me. It was more than one pair of shoes, and they were following me in the dark. I'd planned on letting Beau out of the duffel as soon as I was away from the restaurant, but I kept walking.

I snuck a look over my shoulder. There were four or five of them. In the dark, they were just shadows following me. There was a low voice, some laughs. By the way they moved and sounded, I could tell they were teenagers.

The direction I'd chosen was dark. The bar — the one my fake dad was at — was the other way, and ahead of me were only boarded-up buildings and vacant lots. My anger was gone now. I walked faster.

I heard a voice again, close enough this time that I could almost hear the words. There was an ugliness to the voice, half growl and half laugh. It was a voice that sounded like it was licking its lips. Beau wiggled in the duffel. I switched him to the other hand and tried to go faster. The pills had taken the edge off my headache but they'd left my brain foggy and my stomach sick. I took deep breaths of the cool air to try and clear my thoughts and calm my belly. It didn't work.

I got to another street, as empty and dark as the one I was on. To my left, a couple of blocks down, I could see some lights, some traffic. I turned and made my feet move faster. I was almost running. I looked over my shoulder, not bothering to be sneaky about it. They'd turned, too.

Ahead was a lone streetlight, casting a yellow circle of light onto the cracked sidewalk. It was only a good baseball throw away, but it looked like forever with darkness all around and wolves behind me. I kept my eyes on the light and ignored my heaving lungs, my queasy stomach. I heard another laugh. It sounded like it was right behind me.

You've just got to make it to the light, I told myself.

It was a stupid thing to think. That's the truth.

"Hey! Where you going?"

The voice was scratchy and taunting. I didn't stop, didn't dare look back.

"Why you walking so fast? We can't keep up!" It was a different voice, just as ugly. They all laughed. Beau growled.

"We're talking to you, punk!" There was a little grunt, and a rock whistled over my shoulder and bounced down the sidewalk. It rolled to a stop under the streetlight. I closed my eyes and kept walking. I knew, already, it was no use.

I was fifteen feet from the light when the footsteps started running. I knew from the shakiness in my legs and the burning in my lungs that I couldn't run. And that they'd catch me, even if I could.

They got me just as I stepped into the streetlight's yellow circle. An angry hand spun me around and another one grabbed my shirt. I dropped the duffel.

"What's your problem, you little punk? Why won't you talk to me?"

The face was pinched and pale and angry. It's all I saw. Dark, watery eyes. Eyebrows squeezed down and together.

Red pimples on white skin. A mean mouth, smiling like a shark. Sharp little teeth. His friends were lurking shadows behind him, moving to surround me. They were stupid laughs and shoving hands. They were everything bad and ugly and inescapable. I was alone, with them all around me.

Tears sprang hot and salty to my eyes. It was too much.

"Leave me alone."

The kid snorted. "Leave you alone?"

"Please." My voice, squeezed through my tight and clenching throat, sounded high and whiny.

"Please," the kid said in a squeaky voice, mocking me. His friends laughed.

"Whatcha got in your backpack?" the kid asked, his voice dropping lower and getting more dangerous. I breathed out through my nose and closed my eyes. "You got any money?" I shook my head and tried to say no, but it just came out as a weak moan. My body was so tired. "Oh, I betcha do," the kid sneered. A hand tugged on my backpack. In the duffel at my feet, Beau growled. No one seemed to hear it but me.

The hands pulled harder on my backpack. The straps dug into my shoulders. Mean chuckles and barks of laughter rang out around me. I tried to stand still, to stay on my feet. My stomach turned over and kicked. I swallowed.

"Come on," the kid in front said. "Give it."

I took a deep breath to slow down my lungs.

"No," I said. My anger, chased away by fear, came slinking back. "Go to hell." I gritted my teeth and closed my eyes to hold down the puke.

The first fist hit me in the ribs. I doubled over, my breath gone. Two hands pushed me, hard, from the side. I tripped into two more hands, which pushed me back.

No, I tried to say, but nothing came out.

There was a final, wrenching tug on my backpack.

Another punch, hard and round and sharp, hammered my stomach.

The world fell apart.

I fell.

The sidewalk was hard and sudden, concrete sandpaper that rushed up and smashed pain into my body. A foot crashed into my stomach, another into my back. I started to rise up onto my hands and knees but a fist slammed into my cheek and shot the light out of my eyes.

I didn't cry. But only because I was too scared and sick and hurt to.

My backpack was ripped from my back. I didn't try to stop it. I felt with my feet for the duffel. It was still there. I didn't want them to open it. Beau was a small dog. I knew what they could do to him. I heard the zipper of my backpack buzz open.

"Nothing," the kid's voice said. "Just a bunch of clothes and ropes and crap. Loser."

"What about his other bag?" another voice asked.

"No," I mumbled. Not Beau. "My money. In my pocket." My face was pressed to the sidewalk, but they heard me. Hungry hands felt through my pockets. I felt the lump of my money slip out and away.

"Holy crap," the kid's voice whispered. "There's like a hundred bucks here."

"Leave me some," I croaked, my voice hoarse and my breath short.

"What?"

"Don't take it all. It's mine. Leave me something."

The kid snorted. "I'll leave you something," he said. A hand gripped my shoulder and turned me over onto my back. I opened my eyes in time to see the darkness of the night sky, then the fist flying toward me. It connected with my mouth with a meaty crunch that flashed bolts of pain through my body. My feet kicked out. My shoulders hunched. Blood, warm and thick and salty, ran down into my throat.

The pale face glared down at me, the glow of the street-light behind it. I saw the eyes drop down to my camera, still around my neck. My hands shot up and grabbed it.

The kid pulled at my fingers, tugged at the camera. I held tighter.

"Give it."

"No." I don't know if I said it or just thought it. My body was alive with pain. The kid pulled harder. I held tighter. He shook and yanked and my fingers turned to steel. I wasn't letting go.

He gave a last rocking jerk, and my hat tumbled off. I felt the cool night air on my head.

The kid, his fist clenched back for another punch, froze. His eyes shot up to where my hat had been.

"God," he said. "What's wrong with you?"

I blinked at him.

"You are," I said through my split lips.

His mouth hung open. His fist slowly lowered.

I lifted my camera and took a picture of him.

"Maybe he's got more," a different voice said. I heard a rustling at my feet, where my duffel was. I heard a zipper being drawn back.

Beau was a small dog. But size doesn't tell you anything about how important something is.

Beau came out of that duffel bag like hot burning justice. Like all the right kinds of anger. Like everything the world ever needed. He came out into the darkness and the blood of that cold city street fast and loud and hard, all teeth and bark and bravery.

There were screams of surprise. Shouts. Curses. Shrieks.

"Let's go!" a voice shouted. I heard footsteps slapping quickly away into the night.

The kid who'd punched me was still looking at me. I felt something flutter onto my heaving chest, and then he was gone, too, his footsteps joining the others disappearing into darkness.

I lay on the sidewalk coughing, swallowing blood and feeling all the different hurts in my body. There were plenty. Tears dripped hotly down my cheeks. The sidewalk was hard under my head. Rocks and pieces of gravel poked up at my back. I started to sit up but stopped almost right away; I hurt too much in too many places. I dropped my head back to the sidewalk and looked through tear-blurred eyes up to where the stars should be. There weren't any. Clouds were hiding them, maybe, or they were lost in the lights of the city.

I heard the *click-clack* of claws coming toward me. Beau. I hadn't noticed that he'd left. He'd chased them. Away. And then he had come back to me.

I felt his breath, his sniffing nose, on my hand. Then on my neck, my bloody mouth, then loudly in my ear. I felt his tongue, soft at first and then stronger as he got worried, licking at the blood and tears on my face.

He whined, a quiet but urgent whine, and nudged me with his nose.

I was still breathing. Still staring at where the stars should have been. Still feeling all my hurt, and all my sad.

And my dog was licking the blood and tears from my face.

I turned my head to my dog. Saw his eyes looking into mine, worried. One brown and one green. Felt his sniffing breath again, his warm tongue. A fresh batch of tears sprang to my eyes.

"Oh, Beau," I said. My voice was as scratchy as the concrete beneath my back. My words were blurry and muffled from the blood in my mouth and my split, swollen lips.

He whined again, his breath hot in my face. He was on a dark street in a strange city far from his home. And he was worried only about me. He was my hero.

I reached up painfully, and scratched him behind the ears. His ears dropped and his tail wagged. I brought my hand down to my chest to feel what the kid had dropped there. My hand closed around it and held it close to my eyes so I could see it: a twenty-dollar bill. One of my twenty-dollar bills. I'd had five. He'd left me one.

Here's what I don't get: why people think I need help, just because.

I shoved the bill into my shirt pocket and closed my eyes again, let the tears burn out through my eyelids and down my face to the street.

Beau shifted his paws nervously. He whined.

I knew I should get up. Find a restaurant or some place with a bathroom, get cleaned up.

But I was just too sick. Too sad. Too hurt.

I wanted to die, right there on the sidewalk in a city that didn't care. All of my fight was gone.

I reached out and grabbed the straps of my backpack and the handles of my duffel. I crawled away from the street, away from the light, deeper into the shadows, dragging them with me. My neck, my ribs, my head all protested as I scraped along the concrete. Jolts and jabs of pain rocketed around inside me. The taste of blood in my mouth was strong and bitter.

Finally, I found myself against a brick wall. The lights from the street barely reached me. I didn't think any cars would be able to see me. Good. I didn't want someone to find me. I didn't want anyone to watch me die. I wanted to be alone.

I curled up on my side, facing the wall. Beau stood for a second and then lay down against my back, watching over me. His body was warm.

I closed my eyes and let myself die.

CHAPTER
3½

Sleep hid in shadows.

A friend lost in dark questions.

Rain and wind outside.

Jess lay in bed, the note from her lost best friend clutched tight in her hand. She'd read and reread it enough times now that the words ran through her head without her having to turn on the light to see them. The idea that had tickled and tugged in her mind since Mark's mom first called was alive and in her room with her. She knew, in some deep kind of way, that Mark was not anywhere on the road to Spokane. He never had been. She could feel where he was heading, and her body shivered at the thought. She reached out, through the miles and the storm that wetted and shook her window; she reached out with her heart to her friend, wandering wherever he was. She could feel him, she thought. That was the kind of friendship they had. She could feel his hurt.

"Why?" she asked the darkness. She knew, she thought, where he was going. She knew, she thought, what he was doing. The question that growled in the darkness at her was "Why?"

But there were two wolves growling in the darkness. The one that growled "Why" was followed by a darker, quieter growl that answered. And she liked the answer even less than she liked the question. It chased all sleep out of the room.

She loved her friend. And she didn't know how to help him.

Because the question she wanted to shout back at the wolves in the darkness was this: If she knew where Mark was going, and if she was right about why he was going there — then should she tell?

She needed to know.

Would her best friend choose to die?

What had made him run?

CHAPTER 4

MILES
TO GO:
115

I woke up to the sound of music.

I spit a clot of dried blood out of my mouth and listened.

It was angels, singing. I couldn't understand the words, but it was beautiful.

A warm wind, like breath, blew over my face.

I did it, I thought. *I died*. I licked at my split lip. *It's about time*.

There was nothing but the angels singing, and the warm wind. And lots and lots of pain.

My lips hurt. My teeth hurt. My head hurt. My back hurt. My ribs hurt.

"Crap," I said. My tongue was thick and dry in my mouth. "I'm not dead."

Beau jumped up beside me and panted *good morning* in my face. He whined and licked his lips and wagged his tail so hard his butt shook. He nudged at me with his nose.

"Yeah, buddy," I croaked. My throat was hoarse and scratchy. "Give me a sec."

I blinked and tried to prop an elbow beneath me. Jagged slivers of pain shot up from my ribs to my skull. I managed to sit up and look around.

I was sitting on the dirty asphalt of an alley, tucked into a corner between a brick wall and a green Dumpster. The Dumpster was beat-up and dented, and its smell woke my nose up quick. Somehow I'd managed to crawl behind it. In a sour, foggy flash the whole nightmare came back to me: being followed, the fear, the anger, the rat-faced kid, the beating.

The money.

I fumbled quickly through my pockets and found it. One twenty-dollar bill. That was it.

My hands formed into fists. My breath came hard and fast.

"It's not enough," I said out loud, my voice hard and sharp. Like broken glass. I shook my head. Sickness rose in my belly. My hands went soft. My breaths slowed as I concentrated on not throwing up. I was too sick and too tired to fight back the tears that seeped up into my eyes. "It's not enough," I said again. My voice was small and fragile. Like broken glass.

Beau whined again. His whine opened my ears, and I heard the angels still singing.

Along with the singing voices came another, better smell. It pushed through the reek of the Dumpster. Frying onions. Cooking beans. Grilling tortillas. The smells were spicy and warm and they poked at my stomach with delicious fingers. It smelled like Jess's kitchen when her grandma was visiting from Mexico.

I got on my hands and knees and peeked around the corner of the Dumpster.

There was a door propped open, across the alley. The singing and smells were coming from inside. I squinted at the handwritten sign hung on the door: *San Cristobal's Restaurante. Please Use Front Door.*

Beside me, Beau whined and licked his lips. We both were smelling that food, and I'm sure both our bellies were saying the same thing.

I got to my feet and gasped as the pain in my head roared louder, like someone had turned the volume knob as far as it would go. I squinted and gritted my teeth. Beau was pressed into my leg, his tail thumping against me.

"Stay," I said. His ears dropped, but he didn't follow as I limped over toward the door.

Inside was a narrow hallway crowded with boxes. At its end was the kitchen, noisy and clattering with the sounds of cooking. I could see the backs of three women, stirring and chopping and moving pans around on a couple of giant stoves.

They were the ones singing. They were the angels. A little radio was up on a shelf blaring out some song in Spanish, but their voices drowned it out as they sang along. The song sounded like it was about heartbreak, or hope, or maybe a little bit of both. Their voices rose and fell and rang with emotion as they worked. Their singing and all those sad Spanish words and the sweet spicy smells of the food at their hands all mixed together into something that stuck me right there where I was standing. I leaned my head against the doorjamb and just breathed and listened and smelled. It was something wonderful.

It kinda hurt my broken face to smile. But I did, a little. And I raised my camera and took a picture of those angels cooking that food that smelled like heaven.

But then, of course, the pain in my head and my bones and my face reminded me where I was. And who. And why I was there. I swallowed and blinked and tried to clear the wonderful out of my brain.

There were two doors in the hall, one on either side. Through the one on the right I saw a mirror and a sink and the edge of a toilet. I could feel the dried blood caked on my face. I needed to clean up, and that bathroom would be as good as anywhere else I'd find.

I looked back at Beau. He was sitting with my duffel by the Dumpster, looking at me with his mismatched eyes. He'd lain tight against me all the long night. He'd chased away the wolves and stood guard over me through all the darkness. I blew my breath out and took a look around.

Then I patted my leg and whisper-shouted, "Come on, Beau." He sprang over to my side before I could even smile. "But be quiet," I added as I squeezed through the open door. The sound of the angels got louder.

Their backs were to us, but I knew they could turn at any moment. I hurried to the bathroom and ducked inside, Beau walking tight by my leg with his tail wagging. I caught a glimpse through the door of the other room across the hallway. It was an office or something, with a computer and a phone and a messy, paper-covered desk. Then

I closed the bathroom door and slid the little locking bolt shut.

Beau was loving the kitchen smells. He looked up at me, obviously disappointed when the bolt snapped into place.

"Sorry, buddy," I said. "We're not here to eat. We're just gonna —"

My voice stuck in my throat when I saw myself in the mirror.

My face was scratched up. One eye was surrounded by a puffy black bruise. Another bruise showed darkly on the opposite cheekbone. My lips were cracked and bloody. Between them I could see that one of my top front teeth was chipped. A trail of dried blood trickled out of my nose.

I looked like hell. That's the truth.

I felt things start to crumble inside me. I bit at the crumbling with my back teeth.

"No," I said to the bloody wreck in the mirror. "You don't cry. You don't cry."

And I didn't.

But as I wiped at my face with wet paper towels, my hands shook. Even though I told them not to. And my breaths tripped on their way in and out of my lungs. But my eyes didn't cry. The voices of the angels blew in through a vent above my head and echoed in the room around me.

I took my hat off to wipe at the dirt and blood high on my forehead. I didn't put it back on. I let it drop to the floor and stay there.

I ran my hands over the fine stubble on my mostly bald head. The baldness I was always trying to hide. The baldness that told the world: *This kid's got cancer.* It shouted it. I hated that baldness.

The crumpled postcard was still in the inside pocket of my jacket. The kid hadn't thought to search there when he was looking through my pockets. I pulled it out with shaky fingers.

It showed a mountain. Huge and snow-covered, against blue sky. Printed in curly purple along the bottom were the words *Mt. Rainier.*

I swallowed. That wild mountain — the very top of it — was what I was traveling toward. I'd always known it was crazy. A sick kid, running away to climb one of the biggest mountains in North America. Alone. Yeah — it had always seemed crazy. But there in that bathroom, bloody and bruised, it didn't just seem crazy. It seemed stupid. And impossible. Hopeless. I blinked my burning eyes and stuffed the postcard back in my pocket.

I got all the blood off my face. Even the new blood that came when I wiped the dried blood away. I wiped until my face was clean and the sink was dotted with little droplets of red and the garbage can was almost full of paper towels.

I looked better. But not that much.

And all the while, I thought about the money that wasn't in my pocket. And the food that wasn't in my belly. And the hurt that was all over me. And the mountain I was supposed to climb.

I didn't cry. But I may as well have.

I looked at myself in the mirror, standing there not crying, with my hat on the ground. I looked small. And weak. I looked alone.

I hated myself.

The camera hung waiting around my neck. I held it low in front of my chest and took a picture of my ugly reflection in the mirror. I didn't smile. My skin looked even paler than usual under the flickering fluorescent lights.

"Come on, Beau," I said. "It's time to . . ." I couldn't finish the sentence. I picked up my hat and slipped it back on my head. Beau's claws skittered on the tile floor as he turned with me toward the door. I knew what I had to do. I blew out a tired breath and opened the door and almost ran right into a singing lady walking toward the alley with a garbage bag in her hand. She was tall, with her hair pulled up under a hairnet.

We both stopped. Her voice cut off in mid-song. Her eyes and mouth got big.

She shouted something in Spanish. It didn't sound mean, or angry, or scared. Just alarmed.

She shouted it again, even louder.

The other angels stopped their singing. Then they were there in the crowded little hallway with us. Their surprised eyes took me in, up and down, and then Beau.

I could have run. I should have run, probably. But I was frozen. By my hunger and my hurting. By my loneliness. By the sound their voices had made while they were singing. By the friendly, round shapes of their faces, even when they were surprised by a crazy kid and his dog in their kitchen. By their warm brown eyes that reminded me of Jess.

They whispered to each other in words I couldn't understand. Then the tall one reached forward, slow and easy, and touched the bruise on my cheek. I didn't pull away. Another one stretched out her hand and touched the cut over my eye.

They talked back and forth to each other, their voices rising. They nodded their heads and said kind words into my eyes, words I didn't know.

It felt good. Good to be touched. Good to be cared for.

Then I heard one of them say a word I did know.

Policía.

The word threw cold water on the warmth that I'd been slipping into.

"No," I said, shaking my head. "No police." My brain struggled for the few words of Spanish I'd picked up. *"Por favor."* That meant *please*, I was sure. *"Por favor, no policía."*

Their faces wrinkled in confusion, and they did more urgent whispering back and forth to one another.

I saw the office behind them, across the hall.

I pointed at it, then held my hand up to my ear like a phone.

"Telephone?" I said. "*¿Teléfono?*" I licked my cracked lips. "I want to call — I need to call — my parents. *Mamá*." I said it with the Spanish accent at the end, like Jess did. "*Mamá y papá. Teléfono. ¿Por favor?*"

The worried lines in their faces softened. There was a little more whispering, then they stepped to the side. The tall woman who'd first found me put her arm around my shoulders and guided me toward the office.

"*Sí,*" she said. "*Sí.*" She smelled like flowers and warm food.

I slipped into the little office, Beau coming with me but looking up at them and grinning as he passed, tail slapping back and forth. He's always friendly with people in kitchens.

I closed the door on their watching faces, blocking out their curiosity and the smells of the kitchen. My mouth was watering and my stomach grumbled angrily, but I turned toward the phone on the messy desk.

I fumbled in my pocket for the napkin with the phone number on it. The one from the TV screen in the diner. I picked up the phone.

The dial tone hummed in my ear. In my other ear I could still hear the radio playing. The angels were silent, waiting. I bit at my lip and tasted blood.

With a trembling finger, I started to dial the numbers.

I thought of how sick I felt, how hurt. I thought of the fists and the feet the night before. I thought of all the money that was gone.

I thought of how small and weak I'd looked in the mirror. And I thought of how far I still had to go. My headache was a growling grizzly with sharp claws.

"Washington State Law Enforcement Tip Hotline," a voice blared in my ear. It fought with the aching for space in my head.

"Yeah," I said. My voice barely made it out of my mouth so I cleared my throat and tried again. "Yeah. That missing kid? The one from Wenatchee?"

The next words waited to be said. They waited with the angels' still-silent voices.

"Yes?" the man said into my ear. "Yes? Do you have any information about the missing child?"

"Yes," I said. And I opened my mouth.

But then. But then Beau barked.

Beau almost never barks. He almost never barks. Unless he's mad. That's the truth.

His bark was loud in the little office. I blinked and looked down at him. His ears were pointed up at me, but his tail wasn't wagging. He twisted his head to the side and looked at me. And he whined, just once. I looked into his green eye, and then his brown one.

My head cleared.

Here's what I don't get: why giving up always sounds good until you do it.

Yeah, I was sick and hurt. So what. That was nothing new.

Yeah, most of my money was gone. But I still had some.

Okay, some wolves had torn me up the night before. But then angels woke me up.

Sure, I was all alone. But I had Beau with me. And one Beau was worth more than a whole world full of alone.

I looked up at the clock on the wall. I still had time.

"Excuse me? Do you have any information about the missing child?"

"Yeah," I answered, dropping the napkin into the garbage can. "He's in Moses Lake. I saw him. I'm sure of it."

I hung up the phone.

Beau still stood, looking up at me.

"Thanks, buddy," I said. He wagged his tail and flopped his tongue out of his mouth in a wide smile.

The angels were waiting in the hall when I opened the door. The tall one reached out and pressed something into my hand. It was a warm paper towel, all bundled up. I peeked inside and saw a fresh tortilla, stuffed with rice and beans and onion and red salsa and green cilantro and grilled chicken. The smell that wafted up to me almost made my knees buckle.

Tears burned up into my eyes. Probably from all the spice in the air. I blinked them away like I had in the bathroom.

"Gracias," I said to the women. And once was not anywhere near enough so I said it again, holding the warmth of their food in my hands. *"Gracias."*

They smiled and nodded.

"I have to go," I said, pointing with my chin toward the back door. "My *mamá* . . . she's coming. I have to go."

Even when you're talking to someone who might not know what you're saying, lying to good people just feels bad. But it had to be done. So I did it.

They said some words, most of which I didn't know, and rubbed my shoulders, and bent down to pet Beau. One of them offered him a couple of warm tortillas, which he scarfed down in a few snapping bites.

In the alley outside, I tightened the backpack straps over my shoulder and picked up the empty duffel bag. I held the taco in one hand and knew I'd have to eat it at a jog. I looked down at Beau.

"Come on, Beau. We've got a bus to catch." I took a deep breath, then smiled. "And a mountain to climb."

CHAPTER
4½

Scared. A morning walk.

A question needs an answer.

Knuckles on the door.

Mark's mom answered. She looked like she hadn't slept all night. Jessie rubbed Mark's note between her fingers in her pocket.

"We haven't heard anything, honey," his mom said. "I'm sorry."

"Why did Mark run away?" Jessie asked the question quick, before she lost her nerve. There was no time for "good morning." And it wasn't a good morning, anyway.

His mom's eyes flicked to the side, then back to her. One hand went up to her neck. She licked her lips. And Jessie knew, at that moment. But she still wanted to hear it.

"I know this is hard, Jess. But right now we're just focusing on getting him home safe." Her voice was tired.

"No," Jessie said, shaking her head. "Tell me. I have to know. Why did he run away?"

His mom closed her eyes for longer than a blink. Then she looked out past Jess, out into the daylight world. She sighed out at the sunshine. "Come in, sweetie," she said.

Mark's dad was at the table. Just sitting there, with the phone on the table next to him.

Jess sat down and, after a few false starts, Mark's mom told her everything. She told her about the last call from the doctor and what he'd told her. She told her about how Mark had taken it.

Sometimes crying is easier when someone is crying with you. But sometimes that only makes it worse.

Mark's mom sat looking down at her hands, at her fingers tied tight together. They were a mom's hands, soft, with only small wrinkles, and chipping polish on the nails. They were empty, with only themselves to hold.

Jess sat with her eyes full and down. She hurt. She wanted to stop breathing, because her breaths would not come smooth. They came like tearing paper. She felt, like a broken little bone inside, the loneliness of her best friend. She missed him with the kind of missing that almost feels like anger.

Yes. She knew exactly where he was going. And now she knew exactly why.

He trusted her not to tell. She wanted to reach out and pull him close and slap him across the face.

She felt pinned. Like a butterfly in a case. The eyes were on her.

Before she could try her wings, the phone rang. Mark's dad picked it up. His words were sharp, short. His eyebrows were screwed up tight.

"Uh-huh. Okay. Yeah. Really." He looked over at Mark's mom and shook his head, half yes and half no.

"All right. Yes, of course. Thank you."

He set the phone down and reached out to take Mark's mom's hand.

"Someone called the tip line a few hours ago. Said they saw him in Moses Lake."

His mom gasped. "Well, good!" Her voice picked up new life. "Was there more information? Do they know where to start looking?"

He shook his head. "They don't think it was a real tip. It sounded off. It was a kid's voice. A boy." He squeezed her hand. "A dog barked in the background."

Mark's mom sat with her mouth stuck halfway open.

"Mark," she said at last. Mark's dad nodded.

"They traced the phone call.

"A restaurant. In Seattle.

"They're on their way now."

CHAPTER

5

MILES
TO GO:
113

counted my breaths as I watched Seattle slide away out the bus window. I was panting, and I didn't want anyone to notice me. My legs were still jelly from the run to catch the bus. My body wasn't used to exercise. It didn't like it. The headache was sharpening its teeth on the inside of my skull.

I stretched the fingers of my right hand. They burned from carrying Beau in the duffel. He was still in there, on the seat next to me, between me and the window. I rested my elbow on him softly so he'd know I was right next to him.

"Why you breathing so hard?" A face had popped up over the back of the seat in front of me. All I could see was curly red hair, a freckled forehead, and curious green eyes. I looked around. No one else was watching.

I shrugged. "Just tired, I guess." I looked back out the window, hoping she'd leave me alone.

"Tired from what?"

I pretended I didn't hear her. She leaned farther over the seat.

"Tired from what?"

I blew my breath out through my nose and looked at her.

"From running to catch the bus."

The girl nodded.

"I'm gonna ask my brother if I can sit next to you," she said, and before I could argue, her head disappeared.

The kid sitting next to her looked about sixteen and he pulled his earphone out long enough to say, "Yeah, sure, whatever." In a flash she was squeezing into my seat. I didn't have a chance to fight it. I slid Beau over against the side and pressed in next to him. The girl flopped in beside me, so close I could smell her Doritos breath.

"I'm Shelby," she said. "I'm six."

"Okay."

"What's your name?"

I almost said it, then remembered. My brain scrambled and spat out the first name that came to mind.

"Uh. Jess. Jesse, I mean."

"You going to see your daddy, too?"

"Huh?"

"On the bus. You going to see your daddy?"

"No."

"Oh. I am. It's my first time."

"Your first time seeing your dad?"

"No. It's my first time seeing him at his new house."

"Oh." I looked back out the window. The city was gone now. There were only warehouses and smokestacks and the other cars on the highway.

"My mom and dad got divorced."

"Oh." I didn't want a conversation. I wanted to sleep.

"Jesse?"

I licked my lips and rolled my eyes, then looked at her.

"Yeah?"

"Are your mom and dad divorced?"

"No."

"Oh."

I looked out the window again. Against me, Beau wiggled and tried to scratch at himself in the duffel. I quietly scratched at him through the material. I wished the stupid kid would leave me alone so I could let him stick his nose out and get some fresh air.

"What happened to your face?" Her fingers reached up toward my black eye.

"Nothing," I said, pulling away. I locked my eyes on the whole bunch of nothing out the window. I could feel her still watching me. I clenched my jaw. Maybe leveling with her would shut her up. I turned and leaned down and looked her right in the eye.

"A group of guys beat me up last night," I said in a low whisper. "They beat the crap out of me and took almost all my money."

Her eyes widened. "Why'd they do that?"

I blinked. "Because I kept asking them too many questions."

She thought about that for a minute. "I would've stopped asking them stuff," she said.

I fought it, but a little smile pulled up at the corners of my mouth. "I don't think you would've," I said.

She smiled back. "Prob'ly not. I like talking."

"I noticed."

We sat in silence for a moment. I rubbed a hand up and down Beau's side. He sighed, a sleepy doggy sigh. The sound of the road humming under the bus covered it up.

"If they took most of your money," she asked, "then how'd you get a bus ticket?"

"I already had the bus ticket. I bought it on the Internet."

"Oh." She scratched at a scab on her knee. "My mom and dad got divorced. They just did. We live with just my mom now, because my daddy moved out. This is my first time to go and stay with him at his own house."

"I need to do some work now," I said. I pulled my note-book and pen out of my backpack. The last words I'd written were the ones from the diner, back before the wolves and the angels. I felt like I should write something about the angels. Even if they were only cooks in a noisy kitchen.

I remembered the angels' voices waking me up that morning. I felt for the words, then counted in my head. I started to write.

Waking from nightmares.

"What are you doing?"

"Homework," I said without looking up. I thought, and counted on my fingers, then wrote the next line.

Angels' voices pull me up.

"Why are you counting?"

"Shhh."

I remembered the phone call. I remembered almost giving up. I remembered my sadness turning into anger, and then my anger turning into something else. Something better. I knew what the last line should be.

Leave the wolves behind.

I put the pen down and reread the words. I checked my counting and nodded. God, I was tired. And that weird kind of hungry that doesn't want to eat.

"Why are all your words in bunches of threes?" Shelby asked. She pointed at what I'd just written, and the three lines I'd written in the restaurant.

I was too tired to lie. Too tired to fight. This kid wasn't giving up. And maybe it wasn't that bad to have someone to talk to who wasn't punching me in the face.

"It's a kind of poem," I said, "called a *haiku*. It's always three lines."

"Why?"

"It just is. And the lines always have the same number of syllables."

"What's a syballul?"

"A syllable. It's just a sound. Like this. The first line of a haiku always has five syllables." I read the first line and clapped softly with each sound. "'Wak-ing from night-mares.' Five syllables." She nodded her head. "The second line always has seven syllables." I read the second line, and she clapped with me this time. "'Ang-els' voi-ces pull me up.'"

"Seven!" she said with a big smile.

"Uh-huh. And then the last line goes back to five. 'Leave the wolves be-hind.' It's five, seven, five."

She smiled and ran her finger over the words on the page.

"I like hockey poems," she said.

"It's *haiku*. And I do, too. They're my favorite kind. My friend and I —" My voice stopped when I thought of Jessie. I swallowed and kept talking to fight the burning in my eyes. "My best friend and I love them. Our favorite teacher, in third grade, taught us about them. We use them like a kind of . . . code, I guess. We write notes in haiku. We even talk in haiku sometimes. It's kind of . . . just kind of our thing. Our special thing, hers and mine."

Shelby scrunched up her eyebrows. "Your best friend is a girl? Like a girlfriend?"

"No. Just like a friend who's a girl. We've been best friends forever."

"Oh."

The bus rumbled and shivered around us. I closed my notebook. A man in the seat behind us started snoring.

"When I get there," Shelby said, "I'm not gonna talk to him. Not for the whole weekend."

"What do you mean?"

"My daddy. I'm not gonna say one word the whole entire time."

"Why not?"

Her chin stuck out. Her green eyes started to water.

"'Cause I'm mad. I'm mad. I'm *so* mad." Her voice got a little broken around the edges.

Her fingers were tight in her lap. I could see her anger in her lips. In the red of her cheeks. In her flaring nostrils.

I knew all about anger. That's the truth.

"Wanna take a picture?" I asked.

She blinked. "Huh?"

I pulled my camera out from inside my jacket and held it up. Her fingers relaxed a little. Her eyebrows unscrunched.

"Here," I said. "Smile. I'll take your picture first."

She bit at her bottom lip and squinted at me. I could tell she didn't want to let go of her anger.

"Smile," I said again, and stuck my tongue out at her.

A reluctant smile broke through her frown. I snapped a picture.

"Perfect," I said, and her smile stuck around. "Your turn." I pulled the strap over my head and handed her the camera. She turned it around in her hands and looked at it. Her face screwed up in confusion.

"Where's the screen?" she asked.

I laughed.

"It's not a digital camera. It's an old-fashioned camera, with actual film you have to put in and take out. It was my grandpa's. Just look through the eyehole there and push the button on the top."

She shrugged, then squinted through the camera at me.

"You have to smile," she said, one eye squinched shut as she lined up the picture. I smiled with half my mouth. "And take off your hat."

"No."

She unsquinched her eye at the hardness in my voice. Her smile started to fall down.

"I mean, I don't want to. Go ahead." I smiled with all my face and she smiled back and took the picture.

She stared at the camera for a second.

"How do you see the picture?"

"You don't. Not until you go to the store and get the film developed. It's old school. But it's in there."

"Huh. Do you take a lot of pictures?"

"Yeah. I like it."

"How come?"

I shrugged. "I don't know. I guess I like . . . I like . . . the feeling of catching something. Of saving something." I looked out the window at the trees and signs and the warm houses of strangers zipping past. "It's like, I don't know, grabbing a little piece of life. All this stuff happens, all these little moments go flying past, and then they're gone. And then *you're* gone." I took one long, big breath, and let it out slow to cloud the bus window. "But when you take a picture, that one moment isn't gone. You caught it. It's yours. And you get to keep it."

I looked back at Shelby. She blinked blankly at me.

"Okay," she said.

I smiled and held out my hand. She yawned a big little-kid yawn and gave me back the camera. The bus's tires thumped on the highway like a heartbeat. She dropped her head back against the seat. I unzipped the duffel a couple of inches and felt Beau's sniffing nose poke wetly out. I rested my hand on the duffel, right where his ears were, and let my head fall back against the seat, too. Out the window it was gray and dark. It looked cold.

Shelby yawned again and her head rocked over against my shoulder. I let it stay there. I thought about my mom and dad. A sudden sharp stab of love drilled down into my heart. It was followed by a cold splash of sorry. Sorry for all that I was doing to them. As if I hadn't put them through enough. They'd always done nothing but the best for me. And now I was doing the absolute worst to them. I had to do it. But I didn't have to feel good about it.

"You shouldn't be mad at your dad," I said to Shelby.

"Why not?" Her voice was sleepy.

I shook my head. "I don't know. I think it's just better not to be."

She didn't say anything back. My eyes blinked slower with every car we passed. I swallowed a yawn and let my eyes close. The headache was gnawing on my brain with rusty razor teeth. I thought of the pills in my backpack. But I didn't reach for them.

"Jesse?"

"Yeah."

"You said you're not going to see your daddy. Where *are* you going?"

We zoomed past a green sign on the side of the highway. It said, *Paradise — 110 Miles.*

My stomach twisted around a little red knot of fear.

"I'm going to climb a mountain," I answered.

CHAPTER
5½

Box of old pictures.

Little notes with counted words.

Paper memories.

Jess lay on her bed and looked through the shoe box of memories she kept on the top shelf of her closet. They were mostly pictures of her and Mark, pictures they'd taken together with his old camera. There were the notes, too; the notes they'd passed back and forth in school since kindergarten, the notes he'd left behind the brick under her window. As she looked through them she rubbed at her cheeks and chin from time to time so that her tears wouldn't fall and stain the pictures or blur the words.

There they were, on her first day of kindergarten. Back-pack almost bigger than her body. They were in Mark's room. He was lying in bed. He had to start kindergarten at home, with his mom. He'd been too sick to go to school for most of that year. But they'd still celebrated their first day together. And he'd still wanted a picture of the first day. Like all the other kids got.

A picture of them at the water slides, the summer after first grade. He'd been doing great, then. They thought he might even be better for good. He'd gone to school for the whole year. His smile, with their skinny arms around each other's shoulders, was big and healthy. Just like hers. She liked that their skin looked different — his white, hers brown — but their smiles looked the same. Just happy kids.

Third grade. A party at school, to welcome him back. He'd gotten sick again and had to miss three months. The whole class had made him cards. Mrs. Wilson had them all write him a haiku, because Mark loved haiku so much. In the picture, he looked tired but happy. All the other kids were crowded around him. He had on a baseball hat that was way too big for his head. He was the only kid allowed to wear a hat in school.

Fourth grade. Posing in their soccer uniforms before their first game. They both looked so excited. It had been Mark's best year. He hadn't been sick at all. It was almost like the whole thing had just been some awful, four-year nightmare they'd left behind. There was a note, too, that he'd left in their secret spot at the beginning of that year. Doc said tests look good! his messy handwriting said. *Pizza feast to celebrate. Do you want to come?* Jess sniffed and looked back and forth between the picture and the note.

Next was a postcard, one he'd given her the summer before fifth grade. Mark had gotten so into mountain climbing that summer. His grandpa had been a big-time climber, and he'd given Mark a book about it. Mark had read it over and over. He'd learned everything he could on the subject. Mountain climbing became his secret passion. He didn't tell his parents. They were too overprotective, he said. He didn't tell other kids, because they wouldn't get it; he was too small, too sickly to climb mountains. But he told Jess. He told Jess everything. The picture on the postcard was of a mountain, blue and rocky and capped with a white cone of snow. It looked about a hundred miles high. Under the picture in fancy purple words it said Mt. Rainier. Jess turned the card over, to read the one word Mark had written on the back. Someday.

The last note — other than the one still stuffed in her pocket — was from only a few weeks before. It was short and sloppy. Absent tomorrow. Bad headaches are back again. Doctor wants more tests.

She should have known. Really, she had known. She just wouldn't admit it.

Her eyes burned to a blur she couldn't blink away. But she didn't need to look at the pictures to see Mark's face. She didn't need to read the notes to hear his voice.

She knew, with terrible sureness, what he was doing. But there's lots of kinds of terrible in the world. What he was planning to do was only one kind. And maybe not the worst.

She hated doctors sometimes.

She'd waited at Mark's that morning, waited with his parents for the next call, which they were sure would be the police saying that they'd found Mark at the restaurant and that he'd be home soon. She'd been so relieved.

But then the phone call had come. Mark's mom took the call and then told them both about how the police had found nothing but an empty office and some ladies working in the kitchen. Yes, they'd seen Mark. But they didn't know where he'd gone. There were bloody paper towels in the bathroom.

Mark's dad had shaken his head and closed his eyes. It didn't make sense. Mark was sick, but not the kind of sick that makes you bleed.

His parents had looked so lost and confused and sad. "Where could he be?" they kept asking.

Jess had sat and bitten down on everything she knew. She'd clenched her jaw to hold it all inside her mouth.

Mark had known she would figure it out. He trusted her. It was in her hands.

Should she bring him back, and save him? Or save him, and let him go?

It wasn't fair. To be so sad and so confused at the same time. She had too much to decide, and too much to feel. She was lost.

What should a friend do?

How to help, when helping and
hurting are the same?

CHAPTER

6

MILES
TO GO:
39

The bus rumbled to a stop in a gravel parking lot just off the road.

"Elbe," the driver announced through hissy static over the speakers. "Five-minute smoke break."

The door at the front creaked open, and the driver and a couple of other people got out and lit cigarettes.

It was raining. Clouds covered the world from one edge of the sky to the other and they were so dark gray they were almost black. Wind pushed and pulled at the trees.

Shelby was still asleep against my shoulder. But this was my stop. Mine and Beau's.

The last few miles, while she was sleeping, I'd written her a little note. It was in three lines of five syllables, then seven, then five. It was mostly about being mad. Well, about *not* being mad. I slipped it into her hand. She licked her lips and her fingers closed around it and her head rolled back against the seat and off my shoulder. I stood up, grabbed the handles of Beau's duffel, and slid past her and out into the aisle.

Her brother was sitting, looking out the window. Muffled sounds of angry music seeped out from his earphones. I reached over and yanked the closest one out of his ear. His gaze snapped over to me.

"Pay attention to her, you stupid jerk," I said. His mouth stayed open in an O of surprise. I walked off the bus.

The town of Elbe wasn't much. A curve in the two-lane highway. Some wet-looking houses. A crappy motel next to a gas station. An old train car, off the tracks, had been turned into a restaurant. My stomach went back and forth between starving and pukey. I had to try and eat.

Rain drizzled around me, poking at the puddles in the gravel. My head was a broken drum that was still getting pounded with a mallet. I kept one eye closed, my head hurt so bad. While Beau ran around in the shadows of the trees, sniffing and going to the bathroom, I fished the pills out of my coat pocket. The bottle rattled in my hand, promising me a break from my headache. But I knew the pills would make me sick again. Another meal lost down a toilet. And I needed to eat. I needed to be strong.

I chewed on my tongue, then pressed and twisted the lid off the bottle. Before I could change my mind, I flipped the bottle over and dumped it out. The round little white pills dropped like hard, heavy snowflakes. They almost glowed they were so bright in the dark world of the parking lot.

They fell with little splashes into a muddy puddle at my feet.

I'd have to take the pain from here on out. It wouldn't kill me. Well, it *would*, but that was kind of the point. That's the truth.

The waitress in the railroad car was too busy to ask too many questions. I told her my mom was sleeping in the motel across the street, and she pulled a pen out of her hair and asked me what I wanted to eat.

The food was good and I kept it down, chewing through my headache. Beau sat still like a saint in the duffel at my feet. The meal was salty and hot, and I slipped him as many bites as I could.

While I waited for my change, I looked out the train car window through the rain to the gas station. One car was filling up at the pump. A couple of people with big hiking backpacks stood against the wall, just out of the rain. In a little while a shuttle bus would pull up to take people to the mountain. It was the last part of my trip that I wouldn't be walking. According to my plan, anyway. But in my plan I had the fifty bucks for the shuttle ride.

I could ask the hikers to give me some money. But I didn't want to. I was doing this thing, all the way. I didn't need anybody's help. I didn't want anybody's help. And they'd be suspicious, anyway. Why would a kid want to go up a mountain all by himself? You could die up there.

I grabbed my change when the waitress brought it and walked across the street to the gas station. I didn't really have much of a plan. But I knew where I was going. And I knew how to get there. That was my plan.

I leaned against the wall a little ways down from the hikers. They were a younger couple, like in their twenties. They both had long hair and bandannas around their necks.

The guy looked over at me.

"You going to Paradise?" he asked.

"Yeah," I said. I waited for his next question and wondered what lie I'd come up with.

But the guy just nodded.

"Cool, man," he said. "Shuttle should be here any minute."

While we waited in the gloomy afternoon, several more people showed up and joined us. An older couple with no climbing gear but three cameras and a pair of binoculars. A family with two little kids that ran around and screamed. An old guy with a walking stick who was so lean and healthy looking he looked like he could walk a thousand miles without hardly noticing.

I got lost in the crowd. I liked it. I sat down on the ground against the wall and petted Beau through the duffel.

When the shuttle bus pulled up, there was a flurry of activity. Tickets and money were passed back and forth; backpacks were handed over and hoisted aboard. The driver walked around with a clipboard. He looked busy and grumpy.

I picked my moment. He was around the back of the bus, muscling a heavy backpack into the trunk. I grabbed my duffel and slipped through the people still standing outside and up the steps onto the bus.

I wanted to sit in the back, away from the driver, but it was only a little half-bus and the only spots with two seats still open were right near the front. I needed room for Beau in his duffel. I plopped down against the window with

Beau on the aisle seat beside me and tried to look unimportant. The rest of the passengers filled the other seats around me.

"All right," the driver called out, climbing aboard and closing the door. "Off we go to Paradise Visitor's Center in Mount Rainier National Park. Gateway to the mountain herself. Hope none of you was planning to climb her too soon. We're at the front end of a nasty storm." The bus engine thrummed to life and lurched into gear. We started moving. "A short stop at Ashford, and then we'll be to Paradise in about an hour."

I'd made it. One little shuttle ride and I'd be at the mountain. I'd be at the mountain. And then . . .

And then.

My stomach knotted up again. I could feel my heartbeat pulsing in my neck. My mouth watered, then went dry. My breaths came short and fast.

I shook my head and blinked hard two, three, four times. My fingernails dug into my palms.

"Screw it," I whispered through tight teeth. "Screw it."

Here's what I don't get: why everyone makes such a big deal out of dying.

Dying and living. It's all such a mess. That's the truth. It made me mad. A sad kind of angry.

Tangled all up in my feelings was a memory. I closed my eyes and held the memory in my mind like a smooth river stone.

I was sick, again. Jessie was visiting me, which was nice. I got so bored and lonely when I was sick. I was in bed, Beau curled up beside me like he always was. My mom, who was normally a total clean-freak about something like a dog in bed, never shooed him down. She let him stay with me, where he belonged.

Jessie said something about me being too quiet.

"Oh, he's always quiet," my mom said, rubbing my forehead with her soft fingers. She was beside me, too, like Beau; she always was. "He's always been so quiet and thoughtful."

Jessie shook her head. We were just little kids still, seven years old. "No," she said in that serious little kid way. "Not like that. More like scared."

Little kids are dumb. They'll just say whatever stupid thing comes into their head, no matter how true it is. No matter how sad it'll make someone's mom.

"Scared?" my mom said with a nervous laugh. Her fingers dropped to my shoulder and gave it a gentle squeeze. "What would he be scared of?"

Jessie's voice got hushed and whispery. "Maybe he's afraid of dying," she said, her eyes solemn and teary.

She wasn't being mean, or rude. She just didn't know any better.

But I heard my mom swallow, saw her head jerk a little. I knew that if I looked up, her eyes would be teary, too.

I didn't look up.

My mom started to speak. "Oh, Jess, that's a silly thing to say, that's just —"

But I interrupted her.

"I am," I said. "I am afraid of dying."

My mom's cool fingers rubbed softly on my hot forehead. I could hear her breathing through her nose. I could almost hear words rising into her mouth and then being swallowed back down as she waited for the right ones.

"Being afraid is no way to be, honey," she said at last. "I . . . I know it's hard, baby, but there's no use in being afraid." Her eyes dropped down to Beau in my lap, his ribs rising and falling in his sleep. "Look at Beau," she said. "Do you think he'd let anything happen to you? Do you think he'd ever let you be by yourself or fight something alone?"

"No," I answered in my hoarse voice. "He wouldn't. He's the best. But . . . dogs die, Mom. Dogs die."

There was another silence. My fears and my sadness were all knotted up inside me.

"Yes," my mom responded after a moment. "Dogs die. But dogs live, too. Right up until they die, they live. They live brave, beautiful lives. They protect their families. And love us. And make our lives a little brighter. And they don't waste time being afraid of tomorrow. Look at him now, honey." All three of us looked down at the dog asleep beside his sick boy. I scratched him behind his sleeping ears. "He's not afraid of anything," she continued. "Not worrying about anything. Just living his life, for now. Just happy being here now, with you. He's a good dog."

He *was* a good dog. I reached down and patted him, lying in a duffel on a bus next to his sick boy. Now it was my turn. My turn to live a brave and beautiful life. My turn to live, right up until I died. But I couldn't get my own words out of my head: *Dogs die.*

I was so deep in my memory that I hardly noticed the bus pull over in front of a little hotel and café by the side of the road.

"Ashford, folks," the driver called out, opening the bus door and killing the engine. "Couple minutes here. Some more folks getting on."

I let my head fall back against the seat to wait. I was tired down into the center of my bones. But before my eyes could drop shut, the driver turned and looked right at me and growled through his teeth, "I know what you're doing, kid. Get off my bus. Now."

CHAPTER
6½

A new evening came.

But with it, the same questions.

What should a friend do?

Jessie sat at the table and poked at the food getting cold on her plate. She had no appetite. Her mind, and her heart, were too full of the last two days.

It all hung on her, she knew. On the secret she held, the secret no one knew she was holding. It was a heavy secret. It weighed on her heart like a stone.

Mark's last wish: whether or not it came true depended on whether or not she told.

She knew how torn up his parents were; she knew how miserable their last twenty-four hours had been. She knew how sad and scared and desperate they were. They just wanted their sick son back. Whether or not they got him back depended on whether or not she told.

It was all on her. Her heart shook, holding the secret's heavy weight.

She was going to keep holding it, she'd decided sometime in the middle of the dark afternoon. It was a hard thing for her heart to hold, but her best friend's heart was bearing something far heavier, she knew. And it ought to be his choice. It ought to be his choice.

"Hey, mi amor," her mom said, breaking the silence. "¿Cómo estás? You okay?"

"Sí." Jessie shrugged. "I'm fine, Mamá."

Her mom reached across the table and squeezed Jess's hand.

"Don't worry, sweetie. They'll find him."

Jessie's eyes dropped down.

"Yeah," she said.

Her mom pulled her hand back and took a bite of food.

"Why do you think he ran away? Seems like a terrible thing to do to his parents, after everything they've been through."

Without thinking, Jessie blurted out her answer. Maybe it was because she was tired. Maybe it was because she didn't want her mom saying bad things about her friend, not then. Or maybe it was because her heart couldn't hold on to the weight of two terrible secrets.

"Because he's dying," she said, her voice flat, her eyes still on her plate.

Her mom stopped chewing with her mouth half open.

"¿Qué? What do you mean?" she asked through a mouthful of food.

Jessie felt her eyes fill with tears but she blinked them back, pushed them back down inside her to keep her secret warm.

"I mean the cancer's back," she answered, her voice sounding almost mean. "They found out last week, after the tests."

Her mom swallowed slowly and set her fork down.

"Oh," she said. Then, again, "Oh." She cleared her throat.

"But that doesn't mean he's dying, mija. So his cancer's back. He's beat it before. Mark's always been a fighter. You know that."

Jessie dropped her fork to her plate with a clatter. She shook her head and sniffed.

"But he was supposed to be better, and he's not. He was gonna have to go back in for another round of treatment tomorrow." Jessie finally looked up into her mom's wide eyes. "And he was just feeling good again. His hair was just starting to grow back. And now the cancer's back and he has to start all over again." Jessie shrugged and bit her lip. "And so he left."

There was a silence. A clock ticked somewhere in the house, counting down life's moments.

Jess picked up her fork and brought a bite of food to her mouth. She didn't want to say anymore. She was afraid that once she started talking, she wouldn't stop until it all came out.

Then her mom asked her the question she dreaded.

"Where do you think he went?"

Jess swallowed.

Her heart held tight, as tight as it could, to the secret; held it tight so it wouldn't slip from her heart and out her mouth.

"I don't know," she said, her voice quiet and thin.

Quiet and thin because of the secret her heart strug-gled to hold.

It was so heavy.

Her heart's fingers slipped a bit.

But held on, shaking.

CHAPTER

7

MILES
TO GO:
31

id you really think I wouldn't notice? I know how many seats I got, and I know how many tickets I took."

I didn't answer the bus driver. I stood back under the eave of the hotel, out of the rain. My legs were shaky and my hands sweated. I was too tired for this, and I didn't feel good. I squinted at him through the thrumming pain in my skull.

"You live in Elbe, or what?" The driver's voice was cold and impatient. Like having an extra kid on a bus was the worst thing that could happen to a person.

I wasn't in the mood. I glared at him, then rolled my eyes. "Yeah."

The driver shook his head.

"Don't be mad at me, kid. I don't get paid to give free rides."

Thunder rumbled, and a rainy gust of wind tugged at his jacket collar. He looked back over his shoulder at the weather.

"Aw, heck," he said, then looked back at me with a tight mouth. "You got parents or anything to call for a ride?"

I shook my head and tried to look sad and weak. It wasn't hard. Maybe I could get a ride after all.

But the driver just blew his breath out through pinched lips.

"I can't take you up with me, kid. With these new folks and their bags, bus is full. But this darn storm . . ." He licked his lips. "Stay here. They'll let you hang out in the café at the bunkhouse. I'll drop these folks at the top and pick you up on my way back down, and you can ride back to Elbe."

I didn't say anything. Tears burned in my eyes, but my anger was strong enough to hold them there.

"See you in an hour. You're welcome," he said with a snort. Then he turned and climbed back into the waiting bus.

The rain really started coming down as the bus skidded out of the gravel parking lot. That bus was my only way to get to where I was going, and I knew it. Its taillights glowed red in the growing dark. I watched them get smaller and smaller, and then disappear like two little wishes that wouldn't come true.

Shivering in the rain while trying not to cry and throw up at the same time really sucks. That's the truth.

I unzipped the duffel and Beau bounded out, wagging and panting. Everything was being taken away from me, piece by piece and day by day. He was all I had left. The tears beat my anger and dripped down onto my cheeks. I scratched him behind his ears.

"No more duffel for you, buddy," I whispered. "No matter what. I don't care."

Thunder rumbled again. The two-lane highway was empty except for the puddles. I looked up the highway, the way the bus had gone. The sky was a great gray wall of cloud. I knew the mountain was there, somewhere, but I couldn't see it.

"There's no point in going on, Beau," I said, my voice hoarse. I looked out at the rain, at the skies that were getting closer and closer to black. I swallowed and crouched down and scratched Beau behind his ears with both hands. I held on to him like I was drowning. His mismatched eyes looked somehow brighter in the darkness. He was with me. He was always with me. "But there's no point in going backward, either, I guess." I wiped at my cheeks with my sleeve. I sniffed and flashed Beau the smile he deserved. He smiled back, in his toothy, doggy way. His eyes shone with everything good in the world. I lifted my camera and centered Beau's eyes in the frame. I snapped the picture. Beau's tail wagged harder.

I reached down and scratched him behind the ears again. "Come on."

I pulled my fleece jacket out of my backpack and slipped it on. The rain was pouring down around me. I sealed my camera into the ziplock bag I'd brought along just in case and slipped it into my backpack. I looked at the narrow black ribbon of the highway stretching out between the tall, dark pine trees. And, somewhere in the darkness ahead, a mountain lost in storm.

"Let's walk, buddy. We may not make it. But we'll walk until . . ."

My voice got lost in a rumble of thunder. I didn't know what ending I had planned for the sentence.

Road stones crunched under the soles of my shoes.

We'll walk until we get caught?

Beau trotted beside me, nose sniffing at the mountain air.

We'll walk until someone helps us?

A burst of wind chilled down my neck, and I zipped my jacket up higher to my chin.

We'll walk until . . . we die?

The bridge came closer, step by step, through the darkness. The metal girders looked like dull gray clay in the rain. My clothes were soaked. Rain had snuck down my collar and dripped down my back. I was shivering without stopping.

It was dark enough to be night. It was almost nighttime, anyway. The few cars that passed had their headlights on. None of them stopped. I suppose I was glad they didn't. Their insides looked warm as they disappeared, though.

"That bus'll be back any minute," I said through chattering teeth to Beau. He looked up at me, still walking. "If he sees us, he'll stop. We need to get out of sight. And we need someplace covered to spend the night, anyway." When we got to the bridge, I stepped down off the highway and cut through the weeds down to the river that it arched over. The darkness was deepening by the second, and I had to squint to see.

The riverbank under the bridge was dry, but there was no place to sleep. Jumbled boulders crowded the bank. My body already ached enough — I couldn't sleep wedged between two rocks.

I looked out over the river. Out in the white-crashing water, there was an island. It stretched under the bridge, out of the rain. It was small and mostly sand.

A wide, fallen log reached over the foaming water, leading from the bank where I was standing to the sandy island. I chewed my lip and looked it over. It seemed wet but stable.

"What do you think, Beau?"

Beau's tail thumped against my leg.

"All right, then. Let's go for it."

My shoe slipped on the wet bark on my first step, but I caught myself and took a more careful second step.

It was a huge log, with a nice, flat top almost as wide as a sidewalk. I thought I could do it. I just had to take it slow.

Four steps out, I looked back to call Beau. He was standing on the bank, his ears back and his tail down. He whined.

"Come on, boy," I called. "It's not that bad. Really." Beau hopped nervously from paw to paw. I looked him in the eye and dropped my voice lower. "Come on, Beau. We can do this."

Beau hopped up onto the log and followed me. I turned and kept going, step by careful step.

The water roared underneath me. It churned black and white. It sounded loud and hungry.

Halfway across I realized it had been a dumb decision, but I kept on going. I darted a quick look back to see Beau right behind me.

I took another step. Two more. Three, four, five more. My legs were shaking. My stomach somersaulted with sickness and squeezing fear. The headache pressed on the backs of my eyes with rude, sharp fingers.

I risked a look up, away from my feet and toward the island. I was almost there.

A stupid smile snuck onto my face. I was gonna make it.

Here's what I don't get: why people always think they can do something just because they want to.

With my eyes still on the white sand in front of me, the log slipped wetly out from under my right foot. I helicoptered my arms, trying to catch my balance. My other foot slipped.

Through the thunder of the rushing water beneath me, I heard Beau bark. The sky whirled in front of my eyes, then the bridge.

Then nothing but angry water.

CHAPTER
7 ½

A dark storm coming.

Wind whips rain against windows.

Thunder getting close.

Jessie held the phone in her hand and watched lightning flashes light up the distant hills. Through the open window she could smell the rain. The world outside looked cold and dark. Her friend was out there in it, somewhere. Alone except for a little mutt. With the clock ticking down.

Her fingers traced the numbers on the phone, touched them without pressing them. It would be so easy just to spill her secret. She could call the hotline, tell them what she knew without saying her name. His parents would never know she'd known and hadn't told them. Mark would never know she'd betrayed him. And then all the great squeezing twisting that was inside her would be over. And then Mark would be home.

She was the only one who could do it.

Her finger pressed on the first number. The phone's screen lit up, ready for the next number. She swallowed with a dry gulp and pressed it. Then the third number. There was a lightning flash, and at almost the same time a crash of thunder. Jessie jumped and cried out.

A breeze swept in through the window. It carried the scent of the storm.

The burnt-air smell of lightning wafted into the room and brought with it a memory.

From years ago. Third grade. The hospital. Things were just getting bad. His hair was gone; he was weak and sick and tired. She'd visited him whenever she could. He hated missing school. He hated missing Beau. He hated being alone. They'd played cards on his bed with his mom and dad, and they'd all acted cheerful. Even Mark. And then his parents had left the room to grab them all some food from the cafeteria, leaving Mark and Jessie alone.

When the door clicked shut, Mark grabbed her hand so fast and hard she jerked and tried to pull it away. But his grip was hard and hot. She looked up into his eyes and was surprised to see tears there, brimming up and then spilling down his face. She stopped pulling away.

"I don't like to cry in front of them," he said, his voice shaking. "I know how sad it makes them. I don't like to tell them how bad I feel. Or how scared I am. I don't want to do that to them. Do you understand?"

Jessie nodded, though she wasn't sure she did understand.

"It's like a secret," he went on, still crying. "I can't hold it all by myself, Jess. It's too much. Can I cry with you? Will you hold my secret?"

Jessie squeezed his hand. She looked into his green eyes and nodded again. "Yeah," she answered. "I'll hold your secret."

"Always?"

"Always. I promise."

And he cried, into her shoulder. And he told her how bad he felt. And how scared he was. And by the time his parents got back, they were giggling and playing cards again. She'd held his secret. And every time she visited, she held it again. So his parents wouldn't have to. So he wouldn't have to hold it alone.

Then, the summer her parents had gotten divorced. She'd cried every day. Her dad left and moved back to Mexico. Her mom did nothing but mope around and watch TV and drink a bottle of wine each night. Jessie was alone.

Except for Mark. He called her. He came over. He left notes and candies in their secret spot. Jess had spent the night at his house and she'd cried, and it wasn't even embarrassing. He'd cried in front of her before, after all. "It's not fair," she'd sobbed. "You're supposed to be able to count on your mom and your dad. You're supposed to be able to count on them."

Mark had put a hand on her shoulder. "Count on me, Jess," he'd said. "And I'll count on you. We're the ones we can always count on. Right?"

Jess looked out at the storm, out at the new darkness. Even with his life on the line and the whole world looking for him, he'd stopped to leave a note for her. So she'd know. And to say good-bye. Because he knew she would count on him to do that.

She looked at the note, crumpled on the table. She'd read it so many times that she didn't have to read it again to know what it said.

To my truest friend,

I'm so sorry. And good-bye.

Hold my secret now.

She blinked back her tears.

Mark was counting on her now.

She put the phone down.

CHAPTER
8

MILES
TO GO:
29

At the last second, just before my body hit the black water, I gulped one great big breath of air. I filled my lungs, and then the freezing water grabbed my body and did its frigid best to stop my heart.

The water was more than cold. It was ice that moved. It was strong and fast, and there was nothing I could do. I would have screamed, but the cold was squeezing my lungs like a black fist. For one second I saw Beau looking down at me from the log, getting smaller as I rushed away, and then the water spun me and I was gone. The last I saw of him, his front legs were already in the air. He was jumping in after me.

My feet hit the bottom, bumping boulders and scraping rocks, and I realized the river wasn't deep but it was fast and my feet couldn't stop me from being swept away. I saw the island spinning past my eyes; I was still alongside it. If I was carried past it, I was gone. I dug my feet harder, but they could find nothing to hold on to. I flailed my arms wildly, trying to stroke toward the sandy shore. Water rose up and covered my face, and I jerked and kicked up off the bottom with both feet and all my fear. I popped back up into the thundering darkness and finally managed a heaving breath and one wild scream.

In all that terrible madness, I heard a whining in my ear. I felt a tug on my collar. I saw out of the corner of my eye a brownish blur in the blackness. Beau had hold of me. He was trying to pull me to shore. He wasn't letting go.

If I didn't get to the island, we both would die.

I speared my legs down into the water. They found the bottom, and I pushed toward the island with all that my legs had left. My arms swam and pulled, and my legs thrust back down again, and again hit rock and pushed. Beau whined, and I kicked once more, and for the first time I got my shoulders clear of the water for a second, before my legs were washed out from beneath me.

I saw in a flash of lightning the end of the island. It came to a point and I was close to missing it. A fallen log jutted out into the water from its end, and with one more desperate kick I surged closer and stretched out through the fear and choking cold and blackness. My hands hit wet wood, and I grabbed. My body stopped in the water, but the water pushed and pulled and tried to drag me back down. My feet punched down and the bottom was closer now and I crawled and kicked toward the sand. I felt Beau paddling beside me, his teeth still holding on to my shirt.

There was one last stumbling splash, and then we tumbled together over the log and onto the soft sand.

My lungs heaved and shuddered from the struggle and from the frigid water. Beau stood beside me, panting and shaking the river from his fur.

I shivered like I never had before. Violent, giant shivers that shook me like a car wreck.

I tried to think. My backpack was still on my back, pressed against the sand. My duffel was gone, yanked away by the hungry water.

My teeth clattered against each other, letting my breaths out in a shaky hiss. I was out of the water, but I was wet and freezing. I could still die. Cold, hard rain pelted my face.

I wiggled out of my backpack and fumbled with the zipper. My hands shook and my fingers wouldn't listen to what my brain told them. Beau whined beside me. The cold closed in around us and dug in with its icy fingers. I felt it poke painfully at my bones.

I got the backpack open and dug through it looking for the other plastic ziplock bag. The one I'd been saving for the mountain. But I needed it now.

I found the bag and pulled it out with shaking hands. Sealed and dry inside was a box of matches, some folded-up newspaper, and a couple of cotton balls. The cotton balls were coated with Vaseline — I'd read that they were the best fire starters that you could make.

Dragging my backpack behind me, I stumbled up the island to the sandy part under the bridge, out of the rain and away from the eyes of drivers. I scraped a flat spot out on the sand next to a giant black boulder and gathered a pile of twigs and sticks and branches, the smallest I could find. There were plenty of washed-up logs and sticks on the island, and under the bridge the wood was bone-dry. It was almost totally dark, but the lightning flashes here and there gave me enough light to do what I needed.

I leaned the littlest twigs together in a tiny teepee over some crumpled-up newspaper and shoved a couple of the cotton balls in. My fingers were barely working by then, but I got the matchbox open and dumped a few out and managed to pinch one between my thumb and a numb finger. I scraped it against the matchbox and it sputtered into flame. I concentrated on holding the match steady and firm. I lit the newspaper in several places, then touched the match to the cotton balls. They burned with a slow blue flame. The flames climbed up and around the newspaper, getting bigger and brighter. They curled around the twigs.

"Come on," I begged through chattering teeth. "Come on. Light." Beau stood pressed against me. He was shivering. We both needed the fire.

I blew gently on the fragile flames and saw one skinny twig start to burn, then another. I quickly leaned slightly bigger sticks on top of them and blew some more. The bigger sticks caught fire, and I smiled. I'd done it.

I stacked bigger and bigger branches on the flames as they grew, until a basketball-sized fire snapped and glowed on my little island. It looked almost cheerful.

But I was still shivering so bad I could hardly breathe, and I was wearing clothes soaked with ice water. I piled on a couple of logs as thick as my arm, and when they caught and crackled into flame I held my hands as close to the fire as I could stand until they started tingling with sharp, painful bolts of feeling. I flexed my fingers and stretched my palms until my hands mostly worked again, then started pulling off my wet clothes.

I got my jacket off, then my sweatshirt, then my T-shirt. I shivered worse when the wind hit my bare skin, but I knew it was better than being in wet clothes, so I went to work on my shoelaces. I got one shoe off then added another log to the fire and got the other shoe off. Next came my socks, then my pants, and then I crouched beside the fire, so close it hurt.

Bit by bit, my body warmed. I could feel the deathly river water drying in the fire's heat. I was still covered in goose bumps, and gusts of wind still chilled me from time to time, but my shaking had calmed to just normal shivering, and my teeth stopped chattering uncontrollably.

I wasn't going to die. Not there, anyway. Not then.

I closed my eyes and let that thought roll over me. I'd fought the river, and the cold, and the darkness — and I'd won.

I looked down at myself, squatting in dripping underwear by a fire under a bridge. I started laughing and crying at the same time. It was mostly a happy feeling.

Beau still stood beside me, drying his fur by the fire. The flames flickered in his one brown eye, and one green. He cocked his head at my strange laughter.

"I was afraid of dying," I said down to him. He whined and licked my bony knee. I scratched him behind his ears. I sniffed at my tears and laughed again. "Here I am, on *this* trip, and I was afraid of dying."

But my crazy smile faded when I saw Beau looking up at

me. There was nothing but love in that dog. Nothing but trust. I swallowed and took a few shaky breaths.

"You almost died, too," I said to him. It felt horrible to say it out loud. To admit what I'd dragged Beau into just because I didn't want to be alone and I knew he'd follow me anywhere. "I'm sorry, Beau. That was never part of my plan. It was never part of it. That's the honest truth."

I kept scratching him behind his ears, long after my fingers got tired and my arm ached.

As if that made up for it.

It was a long night. I kept the fire going strong and stretched my wet clothes out on dead log branches around it. It took hours for them to dry and meanwhile I was almost naked, on an island, in the middle of a mountain storm. I was exhausted down into my very middle. I ate an apple from my backpack and shared a couple of granola bars with Beau. All my mind and body wanted to sleep, but I needed dry clothes to sleep in. I talked to Beau to keep myself awake.

Once, during the darkest hour of the night, I wandered away from the fire to gather more firewood. I looked back at our soggy little camp. The firelight was bright and cozy, flashing and flickering on the sand and the boulder and the logs. Beau was curled up within the circle of light. He looked warm, and happy. All around our fire was darkness and wind and the mad, roaring river. I got a lump in my throat. It was awful and sad and miserable. But it was beautiful. The camera was around my neck and I took a picture of the fire in the storm, the light and the darkness and the brown patchy dog.

When my clothes were finally dry, I threw my last three logs on the fire — big, fat ones — and then laid down next to Beau. The fire snapped and muttered. The wind whistled between the rocks. The river was a never-ending wet rumble. From time to time there was the sound of car tires on the bridge above us.

I was asleep before I could even decide to close my eyes.

In the morning I was stiff and sore and starving — but I was alive, and more determined than ever to finish what I'd started. I'd come too far and survived too much to give up. That's the truth. I looked through my backpack to see what I had left. A couple more apples, some bananas, a few granola bars, and most of a pouch of beef jerky. A bottle of water. And a baggie of dog treats.

"Not much food," I said to Beau, who was scratching sleepily at his ear with a hind leg. "But I don't have much time, anyway. It'll be enough."

Before shoving my notebook into the backpack I opened it up. It had gotten a little wet, but the backpack had kept it mostly safe. Some of the pages stuck together a little but it was savable. I sat on a log and looked around at our little island camp. Beau was lapping up some river water to wash down his beef jerky breakfast. I thought of the night before, of the fire and the darkness and the picture I'd taken, and I wrote:

All the world is dark.
But together we build light;
shared, it keeps us warm.

We crossed carefully back over the log and climbed the bank up to the highway. It was long and empty in the morning light. The rain was just a sprinkle, but dark clouds promised more. Wind slipped its fingers down my collar and up my sleeves. I missed my fire already.

Ahead, where the black road twisted out of sight between black trees and gray sky, was the mountain. I still couldn't see it, but I could feel it more than ever. Like it was watching me. Like it was waiting for me.

"Miles to go, buddy," I said down to Beau with a nod. "Let's do it."

I don't know how long we walked. Miles. Hours. I don't have numbers for it. The days and the cold and the food and the journey had taken their toll on my body. My legs made me work for each step, and my stomach threatened to throw up the little breakfast I'd had. My head was full of a fierce pain trying to push its way out through my eyes. I just looked at the empty road right in front of my feet and put a foot there, then did it again. And again. Beau ambled beside me, tongue out, tail wagging. He looked up at me from time to time, and when he did I tried to give him a smile.

I was lost in thoughts that were as dark as the clouds that hid the mountain. Thoughts of the past years, the seven years since that summer phone call made my mom cry. Thoughts of doctors' offices, hospital beds, nurses with kind voices and sad eyes, cheerful cards from classroom friends. Notes from best friends. I thought about the people I'd left behind. My mom. My dad. Jessie. I thought about my grandpa, who used to make me blush when he called me his hero. He'd given me that silver pocket watch and I'd carried it everywhere. I'd loved it — until things got worse and its ticking sounded more like dark footsteps coming up behind me. I loved the watch until I started hating time. And how it ran out.

And, a little, I thought about what was coming. About what I was walking toward, up ahead there in the clouds. About where I was going, and what I was doing.

I was every different kind of sad there is. And every kind of determined, too. In all that I thought of, I never thought of stopping.

I was so lost in thought I didn't notice when the truck pulled up beside me and slowed down. I saw Beau perk his ears and look over, but I was too sick and too tired to notice the man through the window and how he was looking at me.

I didn't notice until he rolled the window down and the sour-sweet smell of cigar smoke hit my nose. Beau growled.

"Hey, kid," he hollered through the rain. "Get in. And don't bother saying no."

CHAPTER

8½

Another morning.

New light, new day, same worry.

A nightmare that stays.

Jessie had been chased by dark dreams all night and she woke up tired. The bed was warm, and she didn't want to leave it. She didn't want to have to face anything, or anyone.

"Come on, mi amor," her mom said from the doorway. "You should try to go to school today. You won't have to think about it so much. I've got cereal waiting for you."

School. Everyone would know about Mark running away, of course. It had been all over the news. Everyone would act weird. They all knew he was her best friend. Her teacher would treat her different. The kids would all whisper. She'd be completely alone.

God — would they call his name at attendance? Would that be worse than skipping it?

The counselor would probably try and talk to her. The counselor always tried to talk to her. But there was only ever one person she really wanted to talk to.

She was afraid that somehow they would all know. She could hide it from just her mom's eyes, or just his parents' eyes, or the police. But there would be so many eyes on her, all the time.

You can't fit a secret in a backpack.

But worst of all: It would all be without him. He was who she walked to school with. Who she sat next to in class.

Who she shared lunch with. There, with all those eyes and that one little space next to her where he was supposed to be, he would feel so much more gone. And she would feel so much more alone.

A hard fist hit her in the stomach. This is how it might always be now. Every day. With him gone. Forever. Always the empty space beside her.

She might have to face this every day.

But not today. She would give her life one more day to completely fall apart.

"I'm not going," she said when she walked into the kitchen. Her mom opened her mouth to argue but then closed it and nodded.

"All right, baby."

She went back to her bed and lay down on top of the blankets and rolled onto her side. She blinked at the icy rain picking at the windows. The sun was up, somewhere. But from where she was she could see only clouds, black as funeral suits.

Half herself missing.

Empty desk she could not face.

A best friend absent.

CHAPTER
9

MILES
TO GO:
24

The rain was pouring down now. I hadn't noticed that, either, tangled in the mud of my thoughts. The wind had gotten stronger, and colder. The storm was picking up.

"Get in," the man repeated. He had a thick mustache and a white cowboy hat. He had one arm draped over the steering wheel, and he was leaning over the seat to shout out the passenger-side window at me.

I just stared at him and swallowed. Beside me, Beau whined. I was gasping for breath like I'd just run a marathon. My legs ached. Rainwater ran down my back. My head hurt so bad I had to squint one eye.

"Listen, kid, you can't be out in this," the man said, shaking his head. "It's only getting worse, they say. May snow, even. Get in and I'll give you a ride."

I shook my head.

"No, thanks," I said. I'd planned on yelling, but my voice came out raspy and weak. "I'm fine. I'll walk."

The man shook his head again. "You're crazy. You'll catch your death of cold. Where you headin'? Paradise?"

I bit my lip and looked up the road. A blustery howl of wind hit me, and I actually had to shift my feet to keep from stumbling. The raindrops were sharp, angry nails hammered into my jacket.

"Yeah," I finally answered.

"You're crazy," he repeated. "That's miles and all uphill. You'll never make it. Hell, *I* couldn't make it. Hop in."

"I've got a dog," I said.

"That's fine. It's a crappy truck."

"And a knife."

He screwed up his eyebrows.

"Okay. Just don't stab me with it."

I stood there. My brain was too fuzzy to think.

"Look, I get it," the man said, dropping his voice. "You're being smart. But I ain't a weirdo. I'm helping you out, son. You're gonna die out here. Hop in."

All the lessons I'd learned from teachers and my parents told me not to get in the truck. But his eyes and his voice told me something else. *A stranger is just a friend you haven't met yet.* That's something my grandpa used to say. It's a dumb saying. There's lots of bad strangers out there. But I guess just about anything can be true, sometimes.

I opened the truck door with a rusty squeak. I picked Beau up and put him on the big bench seat first, between me and the driver. With my backpack in my hands I climbed up inside and clanged the door shut.

The man nodded at me and put the truck in gear, and we lurched into motion. I kept my shoulder pressed against the door and one hand on the handle, just in case.

"Name's Wesley," the man said, his eyes on the road in front of him.

"Oh, I'm, uh — Jesse," I replied.

The man looked at me out of the corner of one eye. "Pleasure," he said with a little nod.

The truck was warm. The dusty vents blew hot, dry air in my face. Whiny old country music murmured out of the speakers. There was a Styrofoam coffee cup propped up next to the gearshift and a cigar smoldering in a metal ashtray sticking out of the dashboard. The man saw me looking at it.

"Sorry," he said, and ground its glowing tip out. His hair and his mustache looked like they used to be light brown, but were mostly gray now. He had friendly wrinkles around his eyes and mouth. *Smile lines*, my mom called them.

We drove in silence for a few moments.

"So — what business you got at Paradise?"

I licked my lips and looked out the window. The tops of the trees were whipping in the wind. Puddles on the side of the road reflected only black sky.

"Just sightseeing," I said without looking at him.

"Huh" was all he answered.

I let the warmth of the truck cab seep through my skin, into my bones. I'd need it all for what lay ahead.

"That's a good dog you've got there," he said, tickling Beau's head. Beau's tail thumped against the seat.

"Yeah. He's a good one."

"Everybody oughta have a dog," he said thoughtfully, his hand still scratching Beau. "Dogs teach you love and kindness. They remind you what's important." He nodded and took a sip of his coffee. "A life ain't much of a life without a dog in it, s'what I always said."

"Yeah." I let my forehead drop against the cool of the window. All the thoughts I'd had walking had followed me inside. Like ghosts, haunting me. "But dogs die," I said quietly, almost to myself.

The man took another sip of his coffee.

"Sure. Course they do. But their dyin' don't make their livin' worth any less."

I smiled, kind of.

"My mom said something like that once."

"Yeah? Must be a special lady."

"Yeah. She is."

My eyelids were as heavy as my feet had been on the road. My heart, too.

"You're tired."

"Yeah. Sorry."

"Nah. Go ahead and rest if you need to."

I woke up some time later, surprised that I'd fallen asleep. Beau was tucked in beside me, snoring. The truck was slowing down, and the man — Wesley — was rolling down his window. I rubbed at my eyes and squinted out the windshield.

In front of us was a little building, like a ticket booth. A great wooden sign stretched above all three lanes of the road.

Mt. Rainier National Park, it said in bold, capital letters. I could see someone in a park ranger uniform standing in the ticket window. The rain was really pouring now.

"I need to give you money, right?" I asked groggily.

"Nah. You may want to duck down, though."

Without asking any questions I undid my seat belt and slipped down in front of the seat.

Wesley pulled up to the window and slowed way down but didn't stop. I was crouched low enough that I could see the top of the ticket window, but not the person inside.

"Howdy, Sheila." Wesley's voice was low and casual.

"Well, hey there, Wesley. Looks like you brought the weather with you."

Wesley chuckled. "Yeah, I guess. Sorry about that. You have a good afternoon, now."

The truck sped up and the window rolled closed, and I crawled back up into my seat. Wesley had his hand flopped lazily over the wheel.

"You work here?"

"Well, kinda. I'm a biologist for the park service, so I do work in several of the parks up here in the Northwest."

"Oh. Cool."

"Few miles more to Paradise," he said.

"All right." Sharp little fists of fear punched my stomach from the inside. Paradise. Where it all really started. Where it all really ended.

Wesley dug into a paper bag sitting next to him on the seat and pulled out a sandwich wrapped in plastic wrap. "You hungry?"

I looked at the sandwich, and before I could stop myself I licked my lips.

Wesley laughed. "Go on. I ain't got much of an appetite. It's ham and cheese. No vegetables or nothing. Share it with your dog if you want."

My stomach, despite all its sickness and worry, rumbled. In a few miles, a few minutes, I'd be making that last, big hike up a mountain. I needed to eat. I took the sandwich.

"Quite a storm," Wesley said, leaning forward over the wheel to look up and out the windshield. "I pity any fool trying to climb the mountain in the next couple of days."

I didn't say anything. I was thinking about Jess, playing cards for hours with me when I was too sick to leave my bedroom. Holding my secrets for me.

"Would even be hard for any rescue teams to make it up," he added.

I chewed on the sandwich and handed every other bite to Beau. He wolfed them hungrily from my shaking fingers. The country music still leaked softly out of the stereo. It was a lady, singing slow. She sounded sad.

"You're just going up for sightseeing, huh?" he asked. "All by yourself?"

I swallowed a chewed-up lump of meat and bread.

"Yeah." I was thinking of my mom, falling asleep in the chair by my hospital bed.

The wheels beneath me hummed. The rain tapped and pattered on the roof, the windows, the hood. My chewing slowed down, down to the pace of the mournful country song from the speakers. Beau was beside me, and the mountain was getting ever closer, and I wanted everything to never go back and never go forward from there. I wanted all the clocks everywhere to stop.

And, for a slow, warm moment, they did.

"I just come over from Spokane," Wesley was saying. I was only half listening. "Through Wenatchee. Little town there. Other side of the mountains." My ears twinged at the sound of my home but not enough to pull me all the way out of my quiet.

"There's a boy missing from over there."

My teeth stopped their chewing. My last bite of ham and cheese turned to glue in my mouth. I could feel him eyeing me out of the corners of his eyes.

"Yeah?" I said.

"Yup. Went missing day before yesterday. Just disappeared. That whole side of the state is talking about it."

I managed to start chewing again, enough to get the bite down. My stomach went back to its sick churning. My headache, which had almost fallen asleep when I had, woke up and hollered in my skull.

"That's too bad," I said. Wesley nodded and took another sip of his coffee. "Where do they think he is?"

"They're not sure. Spokane, they thought, but couldn't find him there. Thought he was in Moses Lake for a bit. Last I heard they'd thought they tracked him to Seattle, but that's as far as they got. They don't have a clue."

So Jessie hadn't told. She'd kept my secret.

Wesley looked over at me, then back out the windshield. I gave the rest of the sandwich to Beau.

"Kid's got his dog with him, they say."

My hands squeezed into nervous fists. I looked out the window at the slashing rain and didn't say anything back. The windshield wipers swiped back and forth, keeping the storm from blinding us.

"Well," I said when the silence got too heavy. But I didn't have anything else ready to say. I was going to say, *"I hope they find him,"* but it was such a lie I couldn't get it out. I licked my lips and closed my eyes. "I hope he's okay," I finally added.

"Uh-huh. Me, too." Wesley's voice was soft and growly. And thoughtful.

We drove on for five, six minutes without saying a word. I kept my forehead on the cool glass and my left hand on my dog and argued in my mind. He knew. He must know. He was taking me to the police. No, maybe not. Maybe he was the world's dumbest biologist. There's plenty of dumb people in the world. Or maybe he knew and he didn't care.

Here's what I don't get: why anybody would try to stop me. All I wanted to do was die. That's the truth.

"I had a son, once," Wesley said. I concentrated on keeping the sandwich down in my stomach. "Good boy, too. Strong. Funny. Big, loud laugh." My ears listened to his words, but my tired brain was working on something else. A plan. Somewhere near the top, I'd say I had to go to the bathroom. He'd pull over and let me out. It was dark, with the clouds and the storm.

"He joined the army so he could go to college. Smart kid. There weren't nothing I wouldn't do for that boy."

I'd go behind some trees and run, me and Beau. By the time he started following, if he even did, we'd be long gone. I nodded, against the glass.

"When he got sent to Iraq it about killed me. I ain't really the worrying type, but I swear I didn't sleep a full night from the moment he shipped out. He was just so *far away*. I couldn't help him. I couldn't do anything for him. I couldn't take care of my boy."

It would mean more walking. A longer climb. But if I waited until we were almost there, it wouldn't be that much more. And it was my only choice. Wesley knew exactly who I was. I was going to have to escape.

I noticed that Wesley had stopped talking. I looked over at him. His jaw was clenched tight, his eyebrows pinched together. I could see his bottom lip shaking, just a little. But his voice, when he spoke again, was still smooth and low and even.

"And when I got the knock on my door, I knew what it was before I opened it and saw the uniforms there. I knew. And they told me. They told me my boy was dead. Thousands of miles away, dead." I kept my eyes on him, and he kept his eyes on the road. His were wet. His next words weren't quite so smooth, not quite as low and even. "A daddy is supposed to keep his kids safe. He's supposed to protect them. That's all there is to it. That's the truth. And I couldn't help my boy." He breathed in and out through his nose.

"I'm sorry," I said.

He nodded. "Me, too." He looked away, out the other window, and took a deep breath and then faced forward again.

"I saw Mark's parents on the news. The missing kid's, I mean."

I almost flinched at the sound of my own name.

"They sure looked scared. And sad. I felt real bad for 'em."

I swallowed, then swallowed again. I knew I had to be sad or mad. One or the other. I made my choice.

I dug my fingernails into my palms. I curled my toes into tight angry balls in my shoes.

"I bet he's fine," I said, and my voice was as hard and mad as the storm outside. "I bet he's just fine and doesn't need anybody's help."

Wesley raised his eyebrows and pursed his lips. He tilted his head to the side in a little shrug.

"Maybe. Or maybe not." He licked his lips, and his voice dropped down. "Thing is, they just announced that this kid is sick."

The last word hung in the warm truck air like a rough poke with a sharp finger.

"Got cancer, apparently."

I breathed tight breaths through my nostrils and gritted my teeth together. I hate the word *sick*. I hate the word *cancer*.

"Had it awhile, they say. Fought it hard. Thought he had it licked. But then . . ." Wesley's voice broke off and he took a breath. "Well, they say it just come back. Recently."

I hated the way he said that. It was the tone of voice people use to say crappy things like *I'm so sorry*.

"That's too bad," I said. Trees zoomed past me, black and gloomy in the storm light. I tried to look at each one.

"Yeah. It's too bad. But the docs say he's still got a shot. He might still lick it, they say. But if he doesn't get in soon for more treatment, well . . . well, that'll be it. It'll come back for good. And that'll be it."

I swallowed a bitter lump in my throat.

"That's too bad," I said again, my voice scratchy. My fingers dug deeper into Beau's fur, scratched down into his skin and pulled him toward me across the seat. He stretched up and licked my arm, gently. I spoke in a whisper, but I think Wesley heard me: "But it always comes back."

I cleared my throat and looked over at him.

"They said all that? On the news? They told everybody that?"

"Mm-hm. Just this morning."

My tongue licked angrily at my lips.

"Isn't that personal? Isn't that private? Why is that everybody's business?"

Wesley shrugged.

"I s'pose they were just trying to get everyone looking, let everyone know how serious the problem was —"

"It's his problem," I interrupted, maybe sounding harsher than I meant to. "It's no one else's problem. Maybe they should just leave him alone."

There was more silence. More of nothing but the rain and the tires and the engine and the radio and the sound of us three breathing there together. I rested my head back against the window.

It was Wesley who broke the silence.

"So what do you suppose he's doing, that poor sick kid?"

I wanted to pull Beau up into my lap and bury my nose in his fur and hug him and not answer. But I kept my forehead pressed to the window. And I left my hand resting on my dog. And I closed my eyes.

"I bet he's going off to die," I said. "Climbing a mountain, maybe."

Wesley blew a breath out through his nose, and I think he nodded.

"And why would he go off and do that?"

"I don't know. Maybe he's tired of being '*that poor sick kid*,'" I said, throwing his words back at him. Anger made my words stronger. "Maybe he wants to be the hero for once. Maybe he's had everything else taken away from him. His friends. His family. His future. All the stuff he wants to do. His life. So maybe all he's got left is his death. That's all that he's got. And so he wants it."

"You think he wants it?"

I closed my eyes harder.

"No. But he's got it. And hospitals suck. And treatments suck. And friends watching you be sick sucks. And watching your parents cry sucks. So maybe he just wants to climb a mountain and disappear."

I opened my eyes and looked right at him.

"Maybe that's all he wants. Or at least all he gets. And maybe they should let him have it."

Wesley nodded. He grimaced. Shook his head.

"Life's a tricky thing, idn't it, son?" His voice was pained. "Figuring it all out, I mean. For all of us. We're all in this thing together. But sometimes there's just no knowing which way to go."

I didn't say anything. Sometimes even the right answers sound wrong if you don't like the question. That's the truth.

"So what do you think a fella should do? A fella that maybe finds this kid walking along a road, and he knows what this kid has and he knows what's going on? What should he do?"

I kept my eyes on Wesley's face. My voice was soft. It wasn't angry anymore. I wasn't angry anymore.

"I think he should pick him up. And help him. He should take him where he needs to go, so he can do what he needs to do."

In the speakers, a guitar twanged. A man's voice cried. Outside was rain and darkness.

"I never got to help my boy," Wesley said.

I looked away, back to the storm outside.

"Maybe you can help this sick kid."

CHAPTER
9½

Dark day spent alone.
Pacing, crying, thinking hard.
Somewhere a lost friend.

She watched the news on the TV. Only a quick mention of Mark, a little update before the weather. The phone number to call. She had it memorized.

The bigger news now was the storm. Coming down from the north. Freezing temperatures, high winds, lots of precipitation. A winter storm in late spring, they said. Unusual. Severe. Dangerous.

"Authorities are suggesting that people stay off the roads and indoors," the announcer said. "Only travel if you need to."

There was a map of the state, showing the clouds moving and the snow falling. Snow only in the mountains, they said. That was supposed to be good news. She looked at Mount Rainier on the map. Lost in white.

"Oh, Mark," she whispered to the screen.

She wondered if his parents were watching. She hoped not. They didn't know where he was, but no matter where they thought he might be, having your kid lost in a storm must feel worse.

"It's getting ugly out there, folks," the weatherman continued. "But it's going to get a lot worse."

Jess was struck by a sudden, terrible thought. What if he wanted her to tell? What if he needed her to tell? What *if he was huddled somewhere, shivering and terrified, wondering why she hadn't called for help?*

What if she was supposed to rescue him?

Shivering, searching.

Doubts and fears like clouds and snow.

Lost inside a storm.

CHAPTER
10

MILES
TO GO:
8

We sat in his truck in the parking lot, looking up at the Paradise Visitor Center. It was a huge wooden building with a great slanting roof divided up into parts. Even though winter was long over, there was still some snow in piles around the building. The parking lot was mostly empty.

Up here, up near the end of the road, up near the top of the mountain, the wind was a living thing that shook the truck and snuck through the gaps in the door. The rain pelted the roof. Where it stuck on the windshield I could see it mixed with snow.

We sat in a waiting kind of silence. Wesley kept looking at the visitor center and the clouds and the rain and chewing on his lips. He wouldn't look at me.

"You ever been to Rainier before?" he asked.

"No. I was going to, with my grandpa, but . . ." I trailed off. I sighed, feeling more sad and tired than anything else. "He was a big climber, my grandpa. Always said he was gonna take me up Rainier when I got better. It was this great secret thing we were gonna do together. But just when I got better, he got sick. His kidneys. And he never got better." I blinked slow and tired, remembering. "He was like this big, strong hero, and he just kind of faded away. For months, lying there in the hospital, just getting smaller and grayer and weaker, hooked up to all those tubes. It was like . . . It was like looking at myself. Seeing my future. You know what his last words were to me?"

Wesley shook his head.

"He said, the day before he died, *'I never wanted to die like this.'* And he made me promise. Promise I'd climb Rainier for him." I looked out, up toward where the mountaintop was hiding behind clouds. "Course, he didn't know I was gonna get sick again. But a promise is a promise."

Another gust shook the truck, reminding us of the cold world outside.

"How can I let you do it?" Wesley asked at last, still looking away. "How can I let you go when I know . . . when I know . . ." His voice cut off and he rubbed his mustache roughly with one hand.

I knew it was gonna take a lie to get me up there. I swallowed and looked over at him.

"I'm not trying for the top, sir. I know there's no way. I'm just gonna go up a bit, maybe try to get above the clouds so I can see the top. For my grandpa. Then I'll come right back down and everything'll be fine." I patted my backpack. "I've got everything I need. Gear and food and everything. I know what I'm doing."

Wesley looked over at me, his eyes pained and his face worried. I didn't like doing this to him.

"Please," I said. "I've gotten no choices. For my whole life, no choices. Let me choose this. Let me have this one thing before all my choices get taken away again."

"You could go with a guide, though, son, or I could go with you, or —"

"No. I need to do this. I need this to be mine. This one thing."

"Son, you could *die* up there."

It's funny. Sitting there in that truck with nothing but the mountain in front of me, I was so scared I could hardly breathe. My stomach was flopping like a fish in a net. But I'd never felt more ready. I'd had enough. Of everything. That's the truth.

"I might die anyway," I said. Beau was sitting up, leaning against me. I dropped my nose down to sniff at his fur. "I don't get anything else. Let me climb the mountain. It's all I want. Please."

Wesley nodded. He was nodding to himself, I think. With his eyes still out the window, he reached out and squeezed my shoulder with a heavy hand.

"Go," he said.

"Thank you," I answered. "And don't call anyone, okay? I'll be fine. I don't want to be rescued. I don't want search parties. I don't want my mom and dad worried about me being up there. I'll call them from the visitor center when I get back down, and they won't have to worry anymore."

Wesley chewed on his lip.

"Just a bit, then you come right back down?"

"Yeah," I lied. "Just a bit, then right back down."

The door opened with a rusty creak, and the wind scooped in and wrapped its fingers all around me. Beau leaped over my lap to be the first one out. I slid down to the asphalt and was about to close the door when Wesley's voice stopped me.

"Son," he called out. I stopped, my hand on the door and frozen rain slapping at my face. "I don't know if I can not tell. Maybe I can. But I know I can not tell for at least an hour or two. I know I can give you at least that. Maybe all of it. I don't know."

I nodded. It was the best I was gonna get, and I knew I was lucky to get it.

"All right. Thank you."

I slammed the door and without waiting the truck rolled to a start, moving away from me slow. I could still hear the country music, softly, could still feel the truck's warmth, still smell the hot air and coffee and sandwich and cigar smoke. I knew it might be my last happy place. And I hadn't even been happy.

I lifted my camera and snapped a shot of a green truck and white snow and black clouds and the friendly shape of a good man inside and red glowing taillights, driving away. Leaving me alone.

I turned toward the mountain. It still wasn't there. It wouldn't show itself to me. Hiding in clouds, waiting for me to come to it.

"This is it, buddy," I said. Beau whined and pranced around me. It was freezing.

On the other side of the parking lot, just past the visitor center, was a dark little stand of pine trees hunched down in the wind. I walked over into the middle of it with Beau at my heels.

"Stay," I told him. Beau cocked his head and looked up at me. "I'll be right back." I put the backpack down and turned and walked away. I knew he'd stay. He was a good dog.

The visitor center was huge inside, with high, towering ceilings and great open spaces filled with displays about Mount Rainier. There was a big, 3-D model of the mountain that you could walk all the way around, and exhibits about the plants and animals that lived there, and information about history and climbing routes. I looked at the model, its black stone faces and great white peak, and I felt tiny and terrified and alone, alone, alone.

With the storm coming, the place was mostly empty. Just a few people here and there, in twos and threes and fours. I recognized some of the people from the shuttle bus and tried to avoid eye contact. I was the only person I saw who was all by himself.

Upstairs there was a gift shop. It had books and maps and movies and key chains. And snacks. I dug through my pocket and pulled out the last of my money. Nine lousy bucks. The last nine bucks of my life.

I grabbed a couple of Snickers bars, some chocolate-covered peanuts, a bag of trail mix. There were a few families shopping around, the kids excited and noisy, asking their parents to buy stuff. I moved through them quietly, without being noticed. It was like I was already a ghost. I wanted to ask them to buy me a stuffed animal and then go home with them and change my name and live forever.

The lady at the register rang up my snacks. "Eight-fifty," she said. The lady looked crabby. She was wearing too much makeup. She smelled like cigarettes and she looked at me like she hated me. My headache, always there, scraped its dull teeth against the inside of my skull.

She couldn't be the last person I talked to. It couldn't end like that. My heart trembled at how small and lonely it felt.

"Is there a pay phone?" I asked. My voice was weak, pushing through my pounding head and trembling heart.

"Downstairs," she answered.

I put one of the candy bars back.

"Could I have my change in quarters?"

She almost rolled her eyes, but she gave me my quarters. I walked downstairs.

The phone was in a dark little hallway that led to the bathrooms. There was no one around.

My hands were shaking, and the quarters squeezed in my fist were wet with sweat.

I fed the quarters in one by one. I felt almost too shaky to stand. My head was one big pounding ache. I screwed my eyes shut, trying to remember the number. I only had one shot. I needed to get it right.

I pressed the numbers, one after another. The buttons were metal and worn smooth by thousands of fingers.

With the last number pushed, I pressed the phone to my ear and leaned forward against the booth and closed my eyes. My ear reached out hundreds of miles through the hissing static.

The phone rang.

CHAPTER
10 ½

Dark room of secrets.

She sat alone in quiet.

The telephone rang.

She walked over to the phone and squinted at the screen. It said "Unknown Caller."

"Hello?"

"Hey, Jess."

He didn't have to say his name. The cup of water she was holding slipped from her fingers and clattered to the floor with a splash, but she didn't look down. His voice — that voice she knew so well — her favorite voice — the voice she'd been missing for two days — just his voice, so small and far away in the phone made hot, blurry tears burn into her eyes.

"Mark? Mark!"

He laughed in her ear, a shy little scared laugh.

"Yeah, Jess. How . . . how is everything?"

She shook her head, and she could tell her breaths were too fast and too small. She was going to pass out.

"Everything is crazy, and I don't care — who cares? — but where are you? Are you okay?"

"I'm there, Jess. I'm there."

She swallowed. I'm there. *He didn't exactly say it proud. He didn't exactly say it scared. Like his words couldn't decide what part of his heart they came from. And her ears couldn't decide what part of her heart heard them.*

"Okay. Are you okay?"

There was a long, long silence. She thought he'd hung up, or the line had gone out. Her knees almost folded beneath her.

But then his voice came back. And it sounded like it was turning away. It sounded like good-bye.

"I just wanted to hear your voice."

"Mark —"

"I was just feeling kind of lonely now, and before I left I just wanted —"

His voice fell off a cliff, and she waited. The words before I left hung in her head like black birds on a tombstone.

"Mark —"

"Thanks for everything, Jess. For all of it. You're —"

"Mark —"

He kept talking, soft but fast, kept talking so that her words couldn't fit in.

"You're the best. You always have been. Thanks for it all. And . . . I . . . I love you, Jess. I just — I just love you, that's all."

There was nothing mushy about it. It didn't matter that he was a boy and she was a girl. It just mattered that they were friends. Best friends.

His voice was so thin, across the miles. So skinny and weak and by itself. Her friend had done it. He'd made it that far, by himself. But now he was there.

Her heart soared and broke at the same time. That's the truth.

"Mark, wait!" she almost shouted. "Mark, listen, I need you! I can't —" But the line clicked dead.

The phone went silent.

Only she heard her whisper.

"I love you, too, Mark."

CHAPTER

11

MILES
TO GO:
8

The storm, now, was fierce.

I started up the mountain.

Beau was by my side.

Of course he was. He always was. When I'd hung up the phone and come outside, he was sitting right where I'd left him, by my backpack in the trees, waiting for me. My other best friend.

I pulled my extra socks and my hiking boots out of the backpack and put them on. I left my sneakers behind. I pulled on my two sets of gloves and high-tech winter coat and the thermal hat that covered my face except for the eye-holes and a little mouth slit. I'd lied to Wesley; I didn't have anything close to the gear you needed to climb a mountain like Rainier. All I had was enough to get me started, to get far enough and not come back down. The second part I'd told him was true, though: I knew exactly what I was doing.

I pulled a little black plastic film canister out of the bag. It was about the size of a C battery. I'd already taped it shut and hooked a metal ring through a hole I'd punched in the lid. Inside was a note that explained it all. And an apology to my mom and dad. And my name, address, and phone number. I clipped it on to Beau's collar, next to his tag.

"You're getting home safe, buddy," I whispered, kissing him on the nose. "You have to." He grinned at me and panted.

Beau and I shared some bananas and jerky and trail mix. I unwrapped a Snickers to eat while I walked, and stood up. We were as ready as we were gonna be.

The trail led right out of the back of the visitor center, right out of the parking lot. Like it was nothing. Just a walk through miles of snow and ice and glaciers and boulders and crevasses to the towering top of a sleeping volcano. No big deal.

It was uphill from step number one. There was snow all over as soon as we'd stepped beyond the parking lot, hard-packed from all the feet before mine, but it still slid out from under me a little with every step. It made the walking slow and my breathing fast already, and I was just getting started. Beau scampered around, happy with snow under his paws and a ham and cheese sandwich in his belly. And his boy by his side. He wasn't worried about mountains.

I didn't want to think about anything, so I thought about how the wind was needling through my clothes to my skin. I thought about how my feet were already starting to feel cold from the snow. I thought about how my legs were rubbery and weak. I thought about my sour, shaky stomach that lurched between feeling starving and feeling pukey. I didn't have to think about my head — that grinding, growing ache did my thinking for me.

Yeah. And, sometimes, between steps, I thought about my mom, and how she'd have no one to pull the blankets up on when they fell asleep.

Or my dad, and how he was probably sitting at the dining room table alone, looking at his hands. Like he did for hours when my grandpa, his dad, died.

And Jessie. Sometimes Jessie. And how hard it must have been for her not to tell.

But I tried not to.

When my legs were burning to their limit and my lungs were sucking at the thin mountain air and my knees were shaking and weak, I stopped for my first rest. I leaned down with my hands on my knees and tried to breathe and not throw up. I looked back over my shoulder.

I could still see the visitor center. It didn't even look that much smaller. I shook my head.

"Okay," I gasped to Beau between breaths. "No more looking back."

The higher you go in the world, the harder it gets to breathe. That's the truth. I'd done my research. The higher you are, the thinner the air gets. There's less of the oxygen your body needs. With less oxygen your muscles get more tired, you can't catch your breath, your brain gets weak and fuzzy. Everything gets harder. On really high mountains, climbers bring their own oxygen in tanks. They breathe through masks like scuba divers. It keeps them alive.

I kept going. The wind was coming from behind me. That was a good thing. It was blowing so hard that it almost blew me over sometimes. It was freezing, and loud, and it was peppered with hard, biting flakes of snow — but it was blowing me up the mountain.

I didn't like the shaking in my legs. I didn't like the stabbing in my empty lungs, or the way my stomach squeezed and rolled and clenched. It was too soon. I knew my body was down to nearly nothing. I knew I was weak and sick. But it was too soon. I had too far still to go.

I kept going. All the thoughts I'd tried to stop were raging wild within me now. Faces and voices and memories. All the people I'd miss. Jessie. My dad. My mom. Other people, too, but mostly them. They were the ones who would miss me.

I stumbled, fell to one knee. I knelt a moment, trying to catch my breath in wind that held more snow than oxygen. Beau pressed himself against me. My legs were wet spaghetti. The faces were still frozen in my mind. I held them there tight. And then, in a sudden gust, my sadness turned to cold anger.

They would miss me. But they would be around to miss me. They got to go on living.

Jess had kept my secret. So what. She'd had to keep the secret of where I was going to die — but I was the one who had to go there and do the dying.

My mom would never get to tuck me in, sure. But I would never be warm again.

My dad would sit alone at a dark table. I was going to die alone in a snowstorm.

They would cry when I was gone, but I would be the one who was gone. They had all the tomorrows in the world to start feeling better.

"It's not fair!" I shouted. The wind swallowed my words and blew them to icy dust.

Here's what I don't get: just about anything. I don't get any of it at all.

My anger was strong enough to lift me to my feet and, one raised foot at a time, push me higher into the storm.

I kept going. The storm was fierce, but so was I.

Beau was an angel by my side. All I looked at was the snow at my feet, and he was always there. Snow clumped in frozen chunks in his fur. I could see him shivering when we paused to rest. His tongue hung out the side of his mouth. But he was always there. Trusting me. Following me. My heart burned with black tears when I thought of where he was following me to. So I stopped thinking about it.

I kept going. Really, that's all there is to it. I was so sick I shouldn't have even made it out of the parking lot. But I kept going.

Even though I said I wouldn't, I turned around once and looked back one more time.

The visitor center was long gone. Behind me was a hopeless white emptiness. There was nothing. There was no one.

The aloneness howled louder than the wind.

Louder, even, than my anger.

My teeth chattered.

"Well," I said, dropping to my knees to hug an arm around Beau's shaking neck, "that's it. That's it, buddy. We're gone." Beau nuzzled in against me. It scared me how much he was shaking. He stretched up to lick my chin. I scratched him behind the ears.

I didn't know if tears could freeze. If they could turn to ice in your eyes and blind you. But they felt too hot to freeze.

I turned back to where I was going, still on my knees. The slope climbed away above me, steeper all the time. With the wind and the snow I could only see maybe a hundred feet.

"I wish I could see you!" I hollered up to the mountain, hoping the wind would carry my words to the hiding peak. There was no answer, and no break in the clouds. I got to my feet. I kept going.

All my sense of time and direction was scattered by the wind. There was only up and down, and I was going up. I kept my eyes down on the shadows of the footsteps I was following, of all the climbers and guides before me. The snow was so white, even in the dark of the storm, that I had to squint. I walked sometimes with my eyes closed. It felt a little warmer that way.

I couldn't see the sun, but I knew that it was moving. Something in the shadows or the angle of the dim light told me that noon had come and gone, and afternoon, and that evening was coming behind the clouds. And, after that, night. Darkness. I ignored my lungs, my legs, my head, and walked faster.

I kept going.

For minutes or hours, it's hard to say, I walked. For feet or miles, impossible to measure, I walked. I was too cold to be hungry.

Although I didn't look back again, I did stop sometimes and squint forward. I wanted to see it. I wanted to see the mountain. I wanted to know it was there.

It was always lost somewhere in the clouds ahead, gone.

It was when I had stopped again, on my hands and knees with Beau shivering beneath me, that I saw the climbers. I was peering up to spy the peak when the blowing snow parted for a moment and I saw a line of people. They were small, far away. They were trudging downhill, back down away from the mountain and toward where people lived.

But they weren't coming toward me.

They were off to the side, up on a ridge of snow a little higher than me. There was a deep little valley of snow between us.

I crouched there with my knees and gloves in the snow. I shook my head and tried to think, sucking the weak air in through my chapped lips.

"They're off the path," I said to Beau. My voice was thin and panting. "They're lost."

I wondered if I should try to get to them, try to warn them that they were going the wrong way. It's a big mountain.

If you wander too far in the wrong direction you can disappear altogether. But, no. I couldn't let them see me. A kid, out here alone in this storm on a mountain. They'd thank me for saving them and then drag me back down. I bet they had a guide, anyway, to get them home safe.

Home. Safe. I shook my head and staggered to my feet and kept going.

It was a little while later — or maybe hours, I don't know — that I realized that I wasn't following any kind of trail at all anymore.

I stopped short. The snow in front of me was smooth and windblown. I jerked around and looked back behind me. No footprints. Not even my own.

I stood and wrestled with the air for breath. I'd been walking in a haze. My thoughts wouldn't string themselves together. Shivers wracked my whole body. I had no idea how long I'd been walking without watching where I was going.

I remembered the other climbers, the ones heading back down.

They weren't off the path.

I was.

What direction had they been in?

I looked all around and saw only white. I couldn't see the ridge they'd been on, or the valley between. I couldn't even remember exactly which way I'd been looking when I'd seen them. I was all in circles.

I kept turning and squinting and shaking my head. At my feet, Beau shook himself and whined. No matter where I looked, there was nothing but white. But it was a darker kind of white than it had been before.

Night was coming.

And I was lost.

CHAPTER
11 ½

Waiting gets heavy.

Wondering is like drowning.

Questions haunt and hide.

Jessie waited at the table while Mark's mom finished making dinner. She always ate dinner with Mark and his family on weeknights, when her mom worked late. Only now there was no Mark. "I'm there, Jess." The words ached in her heart. They were like an open scab. She tried not to, but she picked at them. "I was just feeling kind of lonely."

The whole house hung like broken dishes just before they hit the floor.

The TV was on in the kitchen. It was the news again. She could hear the anchorman's calm, careful voice.

There were only two big stories. Mark and the storm. To the people on the news, it was two different stories. Not to Jessie.

She wondered why his mom had it on. Just for the noise? Just to know the rest of the world hadn't forgotten about her lost boy?

Mark's dad was sitting across from Jess at the table. He had the newspaper out in front of him, but she could tell he wasn't reading it. He was just staring. His face looked lost.

Mark's mom brought out two plates piled high with spaghetti and meatballs. It smelled warm and familiar. Jessie wondered if she'd made it because it was Mark's favorite. Like he was just hiding in the backyard and he'd smell it and come right in out of the dark. Or maybe just because it was the only thing she could try and do for him: make his favorite dinner. It's what moms do.

Mark's dad didn't even look up from the paper he wasn't reading.

"You need to eat something," Mark's mom said quietly, squeezing his dad's shoulder with one hand.

"I'm just not hungry," he answered, shaking his head. "I told you that."

"I know, honey. But you need to eat."

He shook his head again and blew out his breath. "I just can't. Not yet."

She cocked her hip and lowered her chin.

"I'm not leaving till you eat a meatball."

His dad glared up at her, but he stabbed a meatball with a fork and popped it in his mouth. His eyebrows kept glaring but the corners of his mouth smiled as he chewed. Mark's mom patted him on his shoulder and walked back into the kitchen.

His dad saw Jessie watching across the table, and he rolled his eyes and winked at her. She smiled back, and they both took a mouthful of spaghetti.

She chewed and she thought, and it all came together with the taste of her lost friend's favorite dinner in her mouth. She saw the four of them, all connected. Her and Mark and his parents. And Beau, too, out there somewhere by his boy's side. And her own mom, even, getting home from work about now to a dark and empty house.

The windows shook with the storm outside, and all they showed was darkness. And in here, there was family. There were friends. There was light and warmth and hot spaghetti and people helping each other. She saw how his mom helped his dad by making him eat. And how he helped her by eating. She saw people, lost and looking. How they help each other.

Even when they don't want to.

Even when help isn't wanted.

On the news she could hear the end of the weatherman's report: ". . . and it's a Winter Storm Warning for most of the state now, folks. Record low temperatures and snowfall in the mountains. This is one for the books. Stay inside with your families; it's where you belong in a storm like this. Back to you, Rebecca."

Warm tears welled in her eyes. She blinked them back. It was time to be strong.

She jumped to her feet.

"Thanks for the dinner," she said.

"I need to go home."

CHAPTER 12

MILES TO GO: 7

All the world was wind.

Snow and cold were all around.

Darkness was coming.

My shivering was so violent now that it hurt. I stumbled forward, my feet numb. The wind blew right through my clothes, even though I was wearing them all now: my coat over my jacket over my sweater over my shirt. It still wasn't enough. The wind was a monster with icy claws that sunk deep into me and wouldn't let go.

Beau floundered in the snow. His paws broke through in places, and he had to jump and bound to keep moving.

The world was getting smaller and louder. It had frozen down to a shadowy circle of snow. Sometimes there would be a gust of wind and the clouds around me would lift and for a moment I could see out, to snow ridges and cloud banks farther away. But mostly I could only see the ground in front of me, my own feet, and the dog who stayed by my side through the storm.

Yeah. I kept going. I don't know why. I wanted to reach the top. The top of a mountain I hadn't even seen yet. I was so weak, just lifting my feet for the next step was almost more than I could do. But I kept going.

There was no trail in front of me. I was lost, completely. But it didn't bother me that much. Trails are for people who are coming back down. The only place I needed to go was up.

"I'm not giving up!" I shouted into the wind. But my words came out as a wheeze, a cough. They were weak and breathless, and the wind snatched them away before the world could hear them. It was only me, and I was freezing to death.

I lurched forward, all strength gone from my muscles. I tried to take another step and found that I couldn't. I struggled to move my leg forward, but it wouldn't budge. I thought I was stuck.

Then I heard Beau whining, and he wasn't beside me. He was behind me. I looked down and saw him, dug into my footprints, his teeth clenched around my pant leg.

"Lemme go," I said, and was scared at how blurry my words sounded. I tried again to move my leg, but he gripped harder. I stumbled and fell down to one knee. "Whatsa matter, Beau?" I gasped. He whined again, and then let go of my pant leg long enough for one high bark.

I knew that bark. It was the one he used when someone he didn't know was coming to the door. The one he used in the dark of night when he heard a sound he didn't like. It was his warning bark.

He barked his warning bark and then grabbed back on to my pants.

I knelt in the snow and tried to breathe and think, but I couldn't do a good job of either.

I turned to peer through the blowing snow up ahead. And that's when I saw the crevasse.

A crevasse is maybe the biggest danger that lurks for mountain climbers. It is, basically, a giant crack in the snow and ice. A long, skinny, jagged canyon that cuts across the mountain. They can be incredibly deep. A crevasse could be only three or four feet across at the top but hundreds of deadly feet deep. Sometimes their tops get covered by snow, like the mountain's laid a trap. If a climber falls in one, it's almost always the end of their story. You plunge down into the darkness, down until the space gets narrower and narrower and you're finally stuck, pinched between two ice walls, far from any rescue. You die of cold or hunger or suffocation, trapped in a dark coffin made of ice. They are a climber's greatest fear.

Mount Rainier is covered with them.

There was a crevasse stretching right in front of me. It was a five- or six-foot gap across the top. I couldn't see the bottom. I was only a step from tumbling down into it. My heart, already racing, hammered in my chest. Between the snow and the near-darkness and my own sick stumbling, I hadn't seen it. I would've walked right into it. If Beau hadn't stopped me.

I sat in the snow and gasped heavy breaths and felt my heart pounding and peered down into what death looked like. It was black and cold and close. I couldn't see the bottom.

I reached back and patted Beau with a cold-clumsy hand.

"Good dog," I puffed, and he let go of my pants. I leaned down and hugged him, pulled his shivering body tight against mine. "Good dog, buddy." He licked at my chin. His tongue was cold and dry.

I fumbled with my coat and my jacket, opened them up and let the icy air inside so I could pull my camera out. My fingers were dead and distant from the cold, but I managed to hold the camera up and out over the yawning mouth of the crevasse. It was death, waiting. It was what I was running from and what I was walking toward. My throat was a hard, cold lump. I pressed the camera button and snapped a picture of death.

My sweater rode up, and the wind bit like a hungry white wolf into my exposed stomach. I let the camera drop back to my chest and pulled my sweater down and zipped my coat back up. Even though I'd been kneeling there for a few minutes, I was still out of breath. My lungs couldn't find enough air up there to hold on to.

I wiggled out of my backpack and dropped it on the snow in front of me. I couldn't feel my fingers inside my gloves and I tried and tried and could not pinch the zipper to pull it open. Finally, I bit it in my teeth and tugged at the backpack with my hands until it pulled stiffly open.

There wasn't much left inside besides my notebook. A couple of bananas, almost frozen. A Snickers bar. A water bottle, nearly full, with a skin of ice on the top. A plastic baggie of dog treats.

I tore the baggie open with my teeth and spilled the treats out onto the snow. Beau snapped them up and crunched them loudly in his mouth. I bit at the peel on the first banana and managed to get it off, and I scarfed down the banana in a few big hungry bites. My stomach was sick and wasted but it desperately wanted fuel and the banana stayed down. I did the same with the second banana. I chewed right through the wrapper of the Snickers and dug into the candy bar with my teeth. It was mostly frozen but still sweet and salty and delicious. I spit out the pieces of wrapper when I could. My dry mouth almost stuck closed with the chocolate and caramel, but I didn't stop until the bar was gone. I almost smiled it tasted so good.

I shook the water bottle to break up the ice on top and gulped it down. It burned my throat. I poured the rest in a shaky stream for Beau and he lapped at it as it fell. I hoped he got enough.

I looked up, past the crevasse that Beau had saved me from. The storm swirled and seethed. The sun, wherever it was, was almost gone now. Night was sneaking in through the wind and the snow.

When I stood up, though, my legs had new strength. I don't know if it was from the rest or the food. But I was ready.

"Here we go, Beau," I panted, pulling the backpack back on. It weighed almost nothing. All it had left in it was a notebook and a pencil and some rope. I had almost nothing left.

I turned and walked to the side, along the gaping crevasse. It was black, and the wind howled across its top. It looked hungry. It zigzagged diagonally up the slope, getting wider and skinnier as I went. I kept one eye on it all the time. Beau walked on the other side of me, away from the crevasse. He kept one eye on it, too.

The world got darker and darker as we walked, like the blackness was leaking out of the crevasse and up through the swirling snow to fill the sky. Step by step, the dull light of the fading sun was replaced with the pale silver of moonlight. I fought my deep shivers and kept walking.

Finally, I came to a place where the crevasse narrowed down to a thin gap only about two feet across. One big stretching step, or a jump. I looked farther up the slope and saw that the gap widened out again ahead. I was on the wrong side of it, and I didn't know how long I'd have to go to find its end. Miles, maybe. And I knew my time was running out.

"This is it," I gasped, bending down to lean on my knees. "We gotta cross here." Beau whined and shifted from foot to foot. He panted and licked his lips and tap-danced in the snow. "I'm sorry, buddy. I don't want to, either. But we got to. That's the truth."

I slid my backpack off and threw it across the gap. It didn't look far.

The crevasse was narrow, but it was still deep. I leaned out and looked down and saw only the blue crevasse walls disappearing down together into blackness. I tried to swallow but my spit was either all dried up or frozen.

I inched one foot forward so my toes stuck out over the edge. I heard Beau grumble behind me in a growl that turned into a whine. I didn't look back at him. My legs shook. Without thinking I pushed off with my lead foot with all the strength my muscles had left and stretched forward with my other leg. The open black mouth of the ice passed under me and I landed on the other side. My feet slipped on the snow-covered ice, but I made it across and I lay for a moment in a grateful, exhausted pile.

"All right, come on, Beau!" I hollered across the crevasse. I turned around and got up on my knees. "Come on, buddy! You can do it! It's not that far!"

Beau kept tap-dancing. He yipped and whined and ran back and forth in the snow. His whole body was shaking.

"This is nothing, buddy! Don't look down! Just jump to me, Beau! Come on, Beau, come!"

Beau tiptoed to the waiting edge. He yipped again, his ears back and his tail down. His front paws snuck up to the very rim. He gathered his hind legs underneath him and lowered his rump, ready to jump. He looked up at me with his trusting, mismatched eyes.

Here's what I don't get: why that dog would trust me and follow me anywhere after I'd dragged him up the mountain in that storm. That's the truth.

Beau sprang. One of his front paws slipped on the ice. He only got half a sideways jump.

His front paws made it across. But his back paws fell short.

He clawed at the ice for a second with his front claws, but there was nothing to hold on to.

Beau disappeared over the edge into the crevasse.

CHAPTER
12 ½

Black rain on windows.

Biting lips to quiet tears.

Fear. And loneliness.

Jessie paced in her room. From wall to wall.

She circled.

It was dark, inside and out. She hadn't turned a light on. She was alone with too much. Her fear. Her aloneness. Her knowing what she had done. And what she hadn't done. It all crowded in around her until there was no more space in the room for it all and she threw open the door and ran down the hall and out the front door and up the street through the sideways rain. She'd left his house an hour ago but now she was running back, against the wind.

She opened the screen door on the front porch, but before she knocked the front door opened and Mark's mom stood there.

"Jess! I was coming to get you. You didn't answer your phone. There was a call!"

"What?"

"Someone called the tip line. We know where Mark is."

Mark's mom hesitated. There was no smile on her mouth, no shining in her eyes. Her face was painted with the dark colors of worry.

"What? That's good, right? It's good, isn't it?"

His mom looked past her at the darkness, the pelting rain, the whipping wind. She bit at her bottom lip.

"No, honey. It isn't."

Rain dripped down her neck.

Her lungs caught at fearful breaths.

Hopeful heart broken.

CHAPTER

13

MILES
TO GO:

6

leaped forward while Beau was still clawing at the ice with his paws. When my stomach hit the ground, his nose was just vanishing over the edge. I slid on my belly, my arms stretched out, my fingers reaching. My cheek scraped on ice like asphalt.

There was no time to scream.

My hands were dead numb, and inside thick gloves. I felt his body dimly, rushing past my clumsy fingers. With every little thing left living inside me I closed my fingers into iron claws and prayed they would find something to hold.

My fingers were too numb to tell me anything. But one arm burned. It burned with a heavy, wiggling weight. Caught.

I lifted my cheek from the ice. The burning arm was lost over the edge, up to the shoulder. I raised my head to see Beau, dangling down over darkness and death. Three of my lifeless fingers were caught in his collar. But barely.

He shook and wrestled, terrified and strangling. His body jerked and twisted. Any more and he would shake himself loose and fall, forever.

I pulled and grunted. The camera still strapped around my neck pressed like a rock-knuckled fist against my chest. My fingers would give way at any moment.

"I can do it, Beau!" I moaned. "I can hold on! I'm not giving up!" Beau still twisted and shook. "I'm strong enough!" I started to pull him up, inch by tortured inch. My arm muscles screamed. A gust of wind bowled into me like a charging bull.

My three fingers, weak and numb, gave out.

"No!" I screamed as Beau slipped from my grasp. He plunged down into the killing darkness of the crevasse.

For a moment our eyes locked. I looked into Beau's eyes, one brown and one green, as his face plummeted down away from me.

Time stopped. Beau hung frozen, motionless, my empty hand still stretched toward him. All the world stopped moving. I was trapped in the moment that I lost my dog forever.

Then, I took a breath. And let it out. Beau still hung there, in midair, looking up at me. A bluster of wind blew a swirl of snow down into the crevasse. And Beau remained, frozen above the endless blackness.

Time wasn't standing still. Only Beau was. I blinked and squinted into the shadows.

Beau was stuck.

The walls of the crevasse narrowed down to a thin gap, a few feet from the top, and then widened out again below. Beau was squeezed between the sides.

My heart froze.

I'd read about this. Climbers have fallen into crevasses and gotten stuck like that before, pinched between the walls of ice. At first they're relieved: They didn't fall all the way down. But then their body heat melts the ice walls, and they slide down a little farther. And they melt the walls again, and slide down farther. As the crack gets skinnier and skinnier and they keep sliding down, the ice begins to squeeze them. To crush them. They slide down until they're wedged so tight they can't breathe. And then they die, slowly crushed between two walls of ice.

"No," I gasped down to Beau's eyes, looking desperately up at me. "No."

Dogs die. But not my dog. Not like that.

Not my dog that exploded out from darkness to chase the wolves away. My dog that pulled me from a river. My dog that followed me up a mountain in a blizzard. My dog that tried to jump over death because I told him to. My dog.

I tried to stretch down but I knew it was hopeless. He was wedged a good six feet down, way past my groping fingertips. Beau whined. He tried to bark, and he slid a few inches lower.

"Hold still, Beau!" I hollered. Then I remembered the rope in my backpack. And Beau's favorite game. Tug-of-war.

I jumped back and grabbed my backpack and opened it up and yanked the coiled rope from inside and dove back to the edge of the crevasse. I circled a few loops around my waist and made sure I had enough slack to reach him and then tied a knot at the very end.

"Okay, buddy!" I shouted down to his terrified face. "Tug-of-war time, okay? Do you wanna play?" Beau whined back and slid a couple more terrible inches away. I dug my knees into the crusty snow as best I could and threw the end of the rope down the crevasse.

It dangled in front of Beau's face. He didn't grab it. I shook it in front of his nose and he jerked his head to keep it away.

"No, Beau! Grab it! Tug-of-war!" My voice was high and panicked. It sounded strange in my ears, like I was hearing some other kid screaming. Beau's eyes dropped even farther into the crack. My muscles shook and my belly tossed and surged. Hot tears sprang into my eyes. "Now, Beau!" I shrieked. "Grab it, boy! Grab the rope! Please!"

The rope bounced in front of his nose. Beau snapped with his jaws and grabbed it. I felt his weight jerk around my waist.

"Yes! Good boy! Good boy! Hold on!"

I started to pull. He wouldn't budge at first but there was no way I was giving up. I heaved back and he slid loose from the ice's deadly grip. Hand over hand I hauled him up, my back and arms stinging, but not slowing for a second. Beau's teeth were locked onto the rope and I prayed he wouldn't lose his grip or let go. When he was almost to the top, a mere foot from the rim, I pulled myself up to my feet in one final lift and fell backward.

Beau's head and front legs pulled up over the ice. Lying on my back, I could see him between my feet, scrambling on the ice with his front paws. I yanked the rope with all that I had left in my arms, and Beau, still clenching the rope between his teeth, popped up out of the crevasse and onto my chest.

I lay on my back, gasping great empty breaths to the sky. Beau shook himself and whined and clambered on top of me. His weight pressed what little air I had out of my lungs, but I didn't push him off. I wrapped my arms tightly around my dog and hugged him and closed my eyes.

"I almost lost you there, buddy," I wheezed into his fur. I felt his tail slapping against me.

"I'm sorry." I said the words, and there were hard tears in my throat. "I'm so sorry." Once I said the words there was no stopping, and I buried my face in my dog's icy coat and I cried, big breaking sobs that shook us both. I tried to breathe between sobs, but the air was so thin I couldn't get much. So I panted and cried, choking on my tears. I was sorry for so much.

Finally, I sniffed and shivered and slid Beau off of me. I rolled over and pulled myself up to my knees. I wiped the tears from my eyes with my sleeve so they wouldn't freeze to ice on my skin. The howling darkness was huge around me. Like the shadow of a giant's foot held just over my head. I knelt in the blackness and the ice and I looked uphill, squinting against the flying ice.

And then, it happened. What I'd been waiting for.

The wind roared to a higher pitch. The snow came sideways and bit with stinging flakes at my face.

And then, a breathless silence. A stillness, like a dream. The blowing gusts of snow gave way. They broke and parted and it was there, huge and beautiful and so close I could reach out and touch it.

I knelt alone in the snow with death all around me, and I saw the mountain.

Not alone. Beau was beside me, of course. And the mountain was before me. White and shining, painted impossibly bright by the moonlight. Shocking, unmovable white against the black of the sky and the storm and the darkness.

Mount Rainier is an awesome mountain. It is fierce and it is proud. It is almost angry against the sky.

My mouth dropped open. My heart fell down into an icy crevasse and came back up flying.

My hands fumbled at the zipper of my coat. I yanked at my clothes and pulled my camera free and held it up to everything I'd been seeking. I didn't know if the mountain, so grand, could fit in the small frame of the camera. But I held it up and I pointed it and pressed my gloved finger on the button.

I couldn't even tell if the picture had been taken. Maybe my finger, so numb inside its glove, hadn't pressed the button all the way down. Maybe the electronics inside the camera had long since frozen in the bitter cold. But I held the camera up and I saw through its little square window the mountain I had come to find and conquer.

It was weird how something could look so close and so far away at the same time. Like I could reach out and touch it, but I could walk all day and night and never get there.

My breath huffed out of me and I dropped a hand to Beau's head. He was standing, as always, beside me.

"I don't want to die," I said. I looked down at Beau and talked through my tears. "I don't want to die, Beau. Not here." As soon as I said it, out loud in the darkness with the hugeness of the mountain before me, all the anger and aloneness that had haunted my heart blew away like the clouds from the mountaintop.

I thought of the waitress at the diner, that first dark night away from home. I thought of how she'd tried to help me. And I'd been too angry. I wished I could go back. I thought of that waitress and her helping, and I lifted one foot up and planted it in the snow.

I thought of the kid who'd beaten me up. Thought of his eyes when he'd seen my head, my baldness. And he'd left me money. It was my money, maybe, but I was a stranger with a bloody face and he'd given something to me that he didn't have to. I set my other foot in the snow and rose to standing.

I thought of the three angels, singing their songs in a hot kitchen on a cold city morning. I thought of their voices and I could almost hear them and almost smell the food they pressed into my hands and I took a step forward.

No, not forward. A step backward. A step down the mountain. A step toward home.

I thought of little Shelby, sitting on a bus on her way to see her daddy. Hurt and angry. But still wanting to make friends with the weird skinny kid in the seat behind her. Two more steps, tripping but still moving down the mountain. Beau stumbled shivering beside me.

I thought of the shuttle bus driver who figured I was a thief but who was going to stop on his own time and give me a ride home. I took another step.

I thought of Wesley. I thought of his lost son, far away and dead. I thought of the sandwich he'd given me and the music on his radio and the smell of cigar smoke and his eyes when he'd dropped me off. I thought of what Wesley had said — *"We're all in this thing together"* — and I kept walking.

I thought of my mom and my dad. Of long nights in hospitals. Of quiet crying when they thought I was asleep. Of brave smiles to cheer me up. I thought of all of it, and I ached with it all.

I thought of Jess. The best of best friends. The faithful visitor. The warmest smile. The sitting beside beds and not having to talk. Just being there. The secret-keeper. I thought of the last words I'd heard her shout as I was hanging up: *"I need you!"*

I didn't have to think of Beau. He still panted beside me. The friend who always was. Who followed anywhere. Who pulled me out of freezing rivers and away from crevasses I didn't see. Who jumped over death to stay with me.

I didn't feel alone on the mountain anymore. Not at all. I could feel them all crowded around me. I had thought I could do it alone. But I couldn't. And I didn't want to.

There's no such thing as alone. That's the truth.

I was breathing as hard as I could — big, mouth-open breaths like a fish in the bottom of a boat. My lungs still felt empty. There was not enough air to hold me up. But I kept going.

I trudged downhill, alongside the crevasse. There was no way I was gonna make Beau jump that again. I'd head down the crevasse until it ended, then go around it. Downhill was the important part.

I wasn't cold anymore. The wind still pushed and pulled at me with slapping hands, and it still wormed up my sleeves and down my neck. Snow still stung my face. My feet and hands and nose were still numb. But I wasn't cold.

And I wasn't angry.

Not even a little bit.

Here's what I get: everything. Taking my weak little steps through the snow down that mountain, I got it all. I thought of all my sickness, all my anger, all my fear. All that was just the darkness, just the storm. I got lost in it. But there's always the other side of the storm. And the people who get you there.

All the world's a storm, I guess, and we all get lost sometimes. We look for mountains in the clouds to make it all seem like it's worth it, like it means something. And sometimes we see them. And we keep going.

I kept going.

For hours, maybe. I have no idea. I just know it got

darker and warmer and I kept going. The wind got so strong it almost blew me down the mountain, but I kept going. I couldn't hardly hold a thought in my head, but I kept going.

Right up until I didn't.

I stumbled a lot that last long march along the crevasse. Every few steps, really. And I just got back up and kept going. But there came a time when I stumbled and lay in the snow with the wind howling over me, and I didn't get back up.

For a while I didn't even realize that I hadn't gotten up. My brain was long-gone from cold and exhaustion and the thin, oxygen-starved air. I'd been walking numb like a ghost with only faces from my memory in front of me. It was only when I felt Beau nudging me with his nose that I blinked and saw that I was lying down. There was enough snow over my outstretched arm that I could tell I'd been lying there for a few minutes.

I squinted into the windy dark. Just ahead, through the snow, I could see a darker shadow. It was a ledge, a little cliff, with a small hollow underneath. I pulled myself up to my hands and knees.

"I need to rest," I told Beau, though my lips were so dead from the cold it just sounded like a groaned mumble. "Just for a little bit."

He whined back. It sounded as weak as my mumble.

I crawled toward the hollow.

Beau walked beside me, so close he was almost underneath me.

I love that dog.

There was a little space, under the overhang, out of the wind. It was probably still bitter cold, but I was long past feeling it. The space just felt soft, and still, and quiet. Beau curled up beside me, right against my side, and laid his head across my chest. He was shivering. I put my arm over him.

I thought about my notebook, but it was no use. My brain couldn't count syllables. And my hand couldn't hold a pencil. And maybe there was nothing more to say.

I tried to fish my camera out from under my layers, but the numbness now was past my fingers and through my hands and starting up my arms. I lay back in the darkness and breathed in the cold, shallow air.

I blinked. Sometimes I blinked for a long time. And memories flashed through my mind. And faces. All good things. Those are what made it through the storm. I smiled in the darkness.

"I almost made it," I mumbled to Beau, though whether I meant to the top or back home I wasn't even sure.

At some point I woke up with a start and realized that Beau wasn't under my arm.

I jolted up in the blackness and looked around. There was wind and there was dark and there was snow. But there was no Beau.

My dog had left me.

I swallowed once, hard and hot.

And I lay back down.

It had been my plan. I would climb the mountain. I probably wouldn't come back. If I died, Beau would find his way back. He was a dog, and a smart one. He would know enough to leave me, know enough to follow our path back down to people who would help him. It was my plan.

But it was still hard. Hard to be left behind. Hard that he left me, there, alone. But I wanted him to go. I wanted him to live. That's the truth.

"Good-bye, buddy," I whispered into the storm. I don't think any sound came out of my mouth. But my lips moved. "Good luck. I love you, Beau."

The wind closed in around me, and the darkness.

I was alone. But not really, at all.

My face smiled through the cold as I thought of my dog climbing down the mountain into open arms, helping hands, warm places. And I thought of him coming home to Jess, to my mom and dad so far away. But so close. Right there with me, really. I smiled through the cold.

And I closed my eyes to die.

CHAPTER
13½

Days pulled out of time.

Those weeks that were a lifetime.

Watching him come back.

Jessie watched the world spin around her in those days after they found Mark on the mountain. TV cameras; doctors; reporters; police; Mark's parents, including her like she was a part of the family. The three of them had driven through the storm and over the mountains, following the path that Mark had taken to Seattle. His mom never put her cell phone down, receiving the updates from the authorities, the search and rescue coordinator, the state police, the National Park Service. She spit the news out as fast as it came in her ear, sharing it with Mark's dad and Jessie.

The rescue teams had gone up, through the raging storm, through the darkness and the danger, and they'd found him tucked in a little empty space under a snow ledge. So close to dead that they thought he was.

But he wasn't. Not quite. Not yet.

Because of the state of the roads he beat them to the hospital in Seattle, flying through the clouds in a medevac helicopter.

Jessie and his parents ran in, escorted by police and shouted at by reporters, and there he was: scary pale and graveyard thin, lying in bed and hooked up to a jumble of tubes and pumps and beeping machines. He wasn't moving. The doctors had rattled off all the things he'd had: frostbite, dehydration, exhaustion, hypothermia, shock. Cancer.

The whole trip had been too much. The sleeplessness. Not enough food. The stress. Without his medicine, for most of it. At the very time that his body was beginning to fall apart.

He lay without waking for days, and all they could do was sit beside him and wait and listen to the words of the doctors.

"He should be dead already," a doctor said once, and Jess had almost punched him. "He shouldn't be dead at all!" she wanted to shout back into his face. "He shouldn't even be sick!" But punching and shouting wouldn't help, and she didn't want them to make her leave. She needed to stay there, with Mark, by his side.

She was there when he finally woke up. His eyelids fluttered and he stirred and then his eyes opened and they found hers, alone in the room with him. His parents were out in the hall, talking to the doctors.

He smiled, a weak smile.

"Hey, Jess."

Jessie opened her mouth, but no breath would come up from her lungs. Like the air was too thin. Her eyes blurred.

"Am I dead?" he asked. He didn't sound scared.

Jessie shook her head.

"No," she answered, her voice a quivering croak.

"Oh," Mark answered, his voice peaceful and soft and only mildly surprised. His green eyes were so calm, and so wet and bright, and his head was so bald against the whiteness of the pillow. "Good."

And that was it. Oh. Good.

But, then, a sudden dark storm in his eyes. He raised his head from the pillow.

"What about Beau? Is Beau alive?"

Jess blinked, and then blinked again. She looked away from Mark, out the window at the sunlight, thinking of Beau. Then she told him.

She told him how the rescuers had started up into the blizzard. There had been a phone hotline tip that Mark had headed up the mountain from Paradise. They hadn't really thought that they had any chance of finding one skinny kid in all that weather, on all that mountain. But she told him how, less than a mile from the parking lot, they'd seen the little brown-and-black dog with the mismatched eyes coming down toward them. Frozen. Shaking. Barking. She told him how when they'd tried to pick him up the dog had run away from them, leading them back up the mountain.

She told him how they'd followed that shivering little dog as he floundered through the deep drifting snow. Even when he'd veered off the trail, they'd followed their guts and stayed with the dog.

She told him how he'd barked to warn them of the deadly black crevasse. How he'd hesitated for only a moment before leaping over the crack, barely making it to the other side.

She told him how they'd followed that little dog right to where Mark lay, curled up and almost frozen to death. She told him how that little dog had limped all the way back to his boy and collapsed right there beside him, his chin resting on Mark's frozen gloves.

Beau hadn't left him behind, she told him. He'd gone for help. And then brought it back.

Mark didn't even wipe at the tears on his cheeks.

"Jess. Did he make it? Is he alive?"

Jess sniffed and wiped at her eyes and smiled.

"Yeah," she said. And then she laughed. "He's alive. They couldn't get him off you. They had to carry him down on the stretcher, right on top of you. The vet's amazed. Says there's no way he should have survived all that." She reached out and grabbed Mark's hand. "But he had to survive it. To save you."

Dogs die, maybe. But friendship doesn't. Not if you don't let it.

Mark was worn down to nothing. His body was withered and wasted away by it all. But his eyes had more life in them than they'd had in ages. He'd found something, up there on the mountain. Something that stayed with him.

"Does he have a chance?" his parents asked the doctor, when Jessie was there and Mark was asleep. His parents were holding hands. "Can he still beat it?"

The doctor had shrugged, but it was a smiling shrug. "I'd say it'd take a miracle," he answered. "But this kid's got a good track record on miracles. My money's on Mark."

They kept the cameras away, and the reporters. He was the big story. The cancer kid who'd run away. The dying boy who wanted to climb a mountain. Some people thought he was stupid. Some people thought he was a hero. Everyone wanted to hear his story.

But only one person did. Only one person heard all of it.

During those days that added up to weeks in the hospital, Jessie sat by his side.

"I want to tell it all to you," he had said. "Everything. And then I want you to tell my story."

Jess had shaken her head.

"I — I can't."

He'd smiled.

"Yeah. You can. You're the only one who could. You were always the good one with words." His smile had faded. "I need you to, Jess. Before I forget it all." His voice had gotten quiet then. "Or in case I don't make it. I need you to."

And Jessie, of course, had nodded. For some things, there is no saying no.

And so they sat in the hospital and he told it all to her. They paged through his snow-stained journal and read the words he'd written. They looked at the pictures he'd taken.

She saw the broken watch on the train platform, and he told her how mad he'd been, mad at his life, mad at the time that was running out on him.

She saw the dirty little diner, filled with light in a dark city. He told her how sick he'd been, how scared, how angry — angry even at a woman trying to give him kindness.

She saw a blurry picture of an angry face with a cocked fist, looking right into the camera. And she heard about pain and punches and money left behind and a little dog that would fight anything to protect his boy.

She saw a picture of a little hallway with three women shrouded in kitchen steam and a picture of a bald and bloody boy in the bathroom mirror, and she heard about the voices of angels and the decision to keep going.

She saw a picture of a little girl on a bus. And then a picture of Mark, hat on and smiling, with the world out a bus window behind him. And she heard about shared poems and anger and about how anger only makes sense when you're stuck in the middle of it.

She saw a dog by a campfire, on a rain-soaked island lost in darkness. And she heard about fear, and friendship, and warmth in the cold. Light in the darkness.

She saw red taillights on a green truck, driving away. And he told her about lost sons that couldn't be helped, and country music, and the confusion of a kind man not know-ing which way was right.

She saw a gaping black crack, waiting to swallow a dying boy and his dog. And she heard how the boy had been saved by his dog, and then the dog saved by his boy.

Finally, at last, she saw a mountain. Glorious. Majestic. Beautiful. And she heard about peace. About love. About how everything can make sense and be understood.

And Jessie listened to every word. And she wondered how she'd ever be able to tell the story. But she knew she would. Because her friend had asked her to.

He never asked her if she'd told his secret. He never asked the police or his parents about the phone call to the tip line. Whether it had been the gruff voice of an old man or the scared voice of a girl. But he knew there had only been one call. And that was enough. Both had known. One had called. They had both tried to help him.

In those long hospital days, Mark and Jessie told each other nothing but the truth. Except, maybe, once.

It was near the end of the story, at the end of a long day. Visiting hours were almost over, and he was tired. His voice was weak, whispery. Like feathers. The question took her by surprise.

"Was I close?" he asked. "To the top, I mean? I wanted to climb it. To reach the top. Did I get close?"

Jessie swallowed and squeezed Mark's hand in her own.

"Yeah," she'd answered, after a few breathless moments. "Yeah, you got close."

There's more than one kind of truth. There's the truth that you can measure, the truth on maps and charts and in books of facts. And maybe in that kind of truth, Mark didn't reach the top. Maybe he didn't even come close. Maybe in that kind of truth he got lost and wandered off the trail and didn't come anywhere close to the top of anything.

But in the other kind of truth, the kind of truth you feel in a deeper place, in that kind of truth the maps don't matter. In that kind of truth the skinny, bald kid with the disease eating away at him and the little brown dog with one brown eye and one green eye made it farther than they ever should have. They made it farther than minds and maps could measure, but not farther than hearts could imagine.

In that kind of truth, Mark totally made it. He made it to the top of every mountain.

What Jessie said wasn't a lie. It was just a better kind of truth.

That night, in the hotel room, Jess started to try and tell Mark's story, like he'd asked her to. She got out a notebook and a pencil and tried to put it all down on paper.

"Mark was sick," she began. But it didn't sound right. It didn't feel right. Beau was sitting beside her, his warm body against her leg. No pets were allowed in the hotel. But they'd been given special permission.

"Mark was so sick he had to go," she tried again. No.

"Mark —" she tried again, but crossed it out immediately. She couldn't tell his story from afar, she realized. She had to tell his story, his way. It deserved that. He deserved that.

She ripped the page out of her notebook and let it drop to the floor.

She bit her lip and took a breath.

She knew what to do. And once she started, there was no stopping. Not until the story of her best friend and his dog was told, and told right. That's the truth.

She put her pencil to the paper and started writing.

"The mountain was calling me," she wrote. "I had to run away. I had to."

ACKNOWLEDGMENTS

I am so lucky and grateful to have had so much amazing support in my writing journey, from so many people. Too many people, in fact, to even begin to name them all here. I'd never forgive myself if I left someone off. So, instead, I'll just say this: thank you. To all of you. To each and every one of you who helped and encouraged and cheered and believed all these years. Whether you're my wife or my daughters or childhood friend or college friend or adult friend or in-law or parent or sister or coworker or teacher or agent or editor or editorial intern or student or boss or cousin or aunt or uncle or grandparent or book designer or writing club member or writing conference organizer or anyone else who has been on my side through this whole thing: thank you. And if you were wondering if I noticed, if I'd remember and include you here, the answer is: yes. I just did. And always will. Thank you.